The Sheikh's Choice

Kate Goldman

The Sheikh's Choice

Published by Kate Goldman

Copyright © 2019 by Kate Goldman

ISBN 978-1-07440-639-4

First printing, 2019

www.KateGoldmanBooks.com

PRINTED IN THE UNITED STATES OF AMERICA

Table of Contents

Chapter 1

"Who are—" Deja's face planted in the hot sand before she could finish speaking. She tried to kick and wiggle for escape but her efforts were futile. She wasn't strong enough. She felt a knee being driven into her back. She cried out in pain. "Who are you? Why are you doing this to me?" she yelled out.

"Quiet," her captor answered curtly. She felt him tying her hands behind her back. Deja tried to wiggle out from underneath him but his body weight was too heavy for her. She jerked her head up and looked around. She saw the few people that were with her being apprehended by her captor's associates. They were a group of men dressed in black clothing and black headdresses. Deja could only assume that they were nomads. She had read about them. They stole from people or kidnapped them in the desert and did God knows what with them! Panic started to settle in. Deja started kicking harder.

"Let me go!" she yelled out. She kicked again and this time she connected with the nomad's stomach. He groaned.

"Stop," he demanded. His hoarse voice was thick with an Arabic accent. In one movement, he picked Deja up and threw her over his shoulder. It was as if she weighed nothing. She was curvy but not heavy. He carried her to his horse. He perched her on the

1

horse with her legs to one side, and sat behind her. Deja's shoulder rested against the nomad's chest. He snaked an arm around her and held her tightly. He held the reins with the other hand and kicked the horse. It immediately started galloping.

Deja could barely see anything. They were going too fast and there was so much sand flying in her face. "I don't have much with me," Deja began to bargain for her freedom. "Just take everything." She coughed a little from the bits of sand that had flown into her mouth.

"Silence," the nomad ordered. Deja felt helpless. She was on the back of a horse with a stranger and there was nothing she could do about it. She tried jumping off the horse but the nomad held her tightly. She tried headbutting him but she failed after three attempts. She wasn't tall enough to throw her head back into the nomad's face.

"Damnit, stop," the nomad barked.

"Let me go, then I'll stop," Deja snapped. He was the one that had practically pulled her down from her camel and wrestled her to the ground and now he had taken her on his horse. He was the one who should stop, not her.

After galloping for some time, they came to a halt at a campsite. There were a few tents pitched. A few more nomads were already there eating and drinking.

They cheered at the sight of Deja and the other hostages. Some of the nomads shouted in Arabic. Deja couldn't understand what they were saying but she could see that they were happy to see the hostages which made her wonder why. What exactly did they want to do with them? The nomad that Deja had been riding with got down from the horse and then helped Deja down. She was reluctant to get off but she didn't have another choice. She had thought of trying to ride off with the horse but her hands were tied and she didn't know how to ride.

"Move," the nomad said to her with a shove. Deja looked at him and frowned. The other nomads laughed at her response but the one that had kidnapped her didn't laugh. He just pushed again. He gestured towards a large tent.

"Bastard," she mumbled under her breath as she headed over to the tent. She got into the tent and found two women already in there sitting on the floor. Deja raised her eyebrows. She sat down next to them. She huffed in an attempt to blow a curl of hair away from her face. "Hi, were you kidnapped also?" Deja asked.

"Yes, a week ago," said one who was a brunette.

"A week?" Deja spat out in shock. The tourists she had been kidnapped with entered the tent and sat down on the floor. There were only six of them besides Deja. It was such a small group. She had had her reservations about touring in the desert with only six other people but the tour guide had convinced her that it was safe. He had been a tour guide for years and nothing had happened to him or his tourists.

"Yes. They took all our money and jewelry and then just left us in here for a week. I thought they would let us go if we gave them all we had," said the other woman, who was a redhead.

"What are we going to do?" said Emma, one of the tourists. Deja remembered her name because she had been talking so much during their short tour.

"I don't know but we can't stay here for a week!" Deja replied.

"Don't even think about trying to escape," said Salim, their tour guide. Deja whipped her head in his direction. "I saw you trying to fight the nomad earlier. Don't waste your energy, these men are strong and brute. Besides we are outnumbered."

"So we should just give up and sit here quietly until they decide whether to kill us or sell us?"

"We can't win against them. You're not from around here, you don't understand."

Deja crossed her eyebrows "Neither do you! You said this tour was safe," she yelled. She was furious. She hated the feeling of being useless.

"Well it's not. Truth is, traveling in the desert is not a hundred percent safe but we have to make a living somehow."

"There's no use in fighting about it now. The reality of the situation is that we are stuck here with no way out," said Emma.

"You're right, we shouldn't fight but we shouldn't give up either," said Deja.

"I've been here a week. I've already come to terms with the fact that I'm never escaping them," said the brunette. Deja shrugged her shoulders and let regret wash over her. She wished that she hadn't gone on the tour. She should have waited for Kara, her best friend. She was also coming to Al Nurat for work. Both of them had been recruited by one of the top oil companies in the world. Deja had been so excited about it and now she was never going to live her dream of working at Beshara Oils. She was just going to die in the middle of the desert with a bunch of strangers. She couldn't even call her family to say goodbye. Deja was both angry and scared.

Suddenly she heard the sound of horses' hooves beating the ground, and then someone shouting in Arabic. Deja jerked her head up. She heard sounds of men shouting and fighting. She could hear things being knocked over. She wanted to poke her head out of the tent to see what was happening but she knew that it wasn't a good idea.

"What is going on out there?" Emma asked.

"I don't know, go find out," said Salim. Emma and the brunette frowned at him for his rude response.

"It doesn't sound good," said Deja.

"It sounds like they're fighting among themselves," said one of the tourists.

"No, it sounded as though others have arrived."

"Other nomads?"

"Someone might have come to our rescue!" Deja's face brightened. Just as she was about to give up! "Help! We're in here!" she shouted.

"What are you doing?" Salim barked at her.

"If someone out there can help us escape, then we need them to know where we are," Deja replied. Salim shook his head.

"You are trying to get us killed."

Suddenly the tent was unzipped and in walked a tall, dark man dressed in navy-blue slacks, a blue T-shirt and black leather hunting boots. Even though his clothes were loose, Deja could see how muscular his body was. He had jet-black hair and a week-old stubble. He stood in the opening of the tent with such a serious expression. He had a very intimidating and demanding presence. Deja hadn't seen him earlier. So, she wasn't sure if he was there to kill them or save them.

"Who are you? Are you here to help us or kill us?" Deja asked. She figured that was the only way to find out. The others turned their heads and looked at her as though she was crazy.

Chapter 2

"I am not here to kill anyone," the man told Deja. He had a husky voice that made Deja a little nervous. She sprang up to her feet and squared her shoulders. If he was there to kill them, she was not going to die without a fight. She was prepared to run, even though she knew that it would be pointless. They had horses. Maybe she could steal a horse, she thought to herself. Her subconscious screamed out that she needed to stop being stubborn and that she needed to just calm down and accept the situation at hand.

"Then why are you here?" she asked him. He stared at her blankly. He was much taller and bigger than her. He could crush her in one go.

"I came to take you back to the capital," he said.

"You're not with them?" Deja nodded her head towards the outside of the tent. "The men that kidnapped us?"

"No." The man shook his head.

"Are you really here to help us?" Emma asked. Her shaky voice matched her trembling hands. The man nodded.

"You all need to stand up and come with me. There is a sandstorm coming. We need to be out of here as soon as possible," he said. Deja raised her eyebrows. A sandstorm? She had heard about them but never thought that she would be anywhere near one.

"Can we trust you?" Deja asked him. He looked at her with an expressionless face.

"It makes no difference to me whether you trust me or not. However, it will not change the situation at hand," he said. Deja frowned a little. The man turned his back to Deja. She couldn't help but notice how broad it was. "Let's go," he said and then started walking towards the flap of the tent.

Deja turned to look at the other hostages. "Do you guys think that he is here to save us?" she asked them.

"I don't know," said Salim as he rose to his feet. "We have no choice but to get out of the tent and find out," he added. The other hostages also stood up.

"You're right," said Deja. She headed over to the flap of the tent and walked out. It was not like they could stay in the tent forever.

Deja studied her surroundings. She saw the man that had kidnapped her on his knees with his hands tied behind his back. She glanced around and noticed that there were a lot of men dressed in navy blue. They were fighting against the nomads.

"Oh, my God," Deja breathed. She placed her hand on her chest as she watched the nomads get apprehended by the men in blue. The men in blue seemed to be stronger and more skilled. The other hostages came out of the tent and stood behind Deja.

"We are going to take you back to the capital," a voice sounded. Deja turned her head and found a tall man standing before her. He smiled at her and then turned his attention to the other hostages. "Don't worry, you are all safe now. We will safely escort you back to the capital," he said to them.

"Thank you so much," said Emma. "We had lost all hope." The other hostages also thanked him.

"Let's go, there is a sandstorm coming. We must leave now," said the man. He turned on his heel and led the hostages towards some of the men in navy blue who were standing by their horses. He allocated one hostage for each rider to take to safety. The tall man that had smiled at Deja held onto the reins and got up onto his horse. He sat comfortably on the saddle and then stretched his hand out to Deja.

She hesitated. She was a bit skeptical about getting on the horse with a stranger. She had had an awful experience earlier. "Are you going to get on?" he asked Deja as he stretched out his hand to her.

"I am," she replied. She put her hand into his and then he pulled her up onto the horse.

"Hold onto my waist."

Deja grabbed onto his clothes. She felt a little uncomfortable about being so close to this stranger but she had no choice. He was rescuing her from the nomads. She had no idea why they had kidnapped her tour group. Were they going to sell them as slaves or keep them as slaves or maybe just kill them? Deja wondered. She was glad that she was not going to find out.

***

Deja and the others arrived at a campsite about half an hour later. They had galloped so fast that sand was flying into Deja's mouth. She was so happy when they finally came to a halt. The man she had been riding with helped her off the horse.

"Thank you," she said to him. She looked around the campsite. There were a lot of tents set up already. There were a lot of jeeps parked around. She crossed her eyebrows as she wondered who those men in navy blue were. Were they policemen or soldiers? They had horses and jeeps, and they apparently had the authority to capture the nomads and rescue the hostages.

"You're welcome," he said. "Are you okay? You were coughing a lot."

"There was too much sand flying in my face," she replied.

"Would you like some water?"

"Yes, thank you."

He nodded and walked off to one of the tents. Deja stood there and waited for his return. The other hostages dismounted from the horses and were taken to a tent.

Suddenly, Deja heard horses galloping. She looked up and saw the rest of the men in navy blue arriving with the nomads in handcuffs. Deja crossed her arms over her chest and watched the nomads being taken to a tent. She saw the tall, handsome man who had walked into the tent and told them that he was taking them to the capital. He dismounted from his horse.

"Here," a voice distracted Deja from her staring. She turned her head and found the man she rode with standing in front of her with a bottle of water.

"Thank you," she said as she took the bottle from him. She opened it and drank half the bottle. She had not realized she was that thirsty. "I'm Deja. What shall I call you?"

"Tariq," he replied with a smile. His soft voice was thick with an Arabic accent.

"Tariq," she repeated. She raised an eyebrow. "So, who are you people? Police or part of the army?"

"Neither."

Deja crossed her eyebrows. She opened her mouth to speak but was interrupted by someone speaking in Arabic. It was that tall man who she had met in the tent earlier. He spoke to Tariq and then walked off.

He did not even look at Deja nor did he say anything to her. He had a cold demeanor.

"Go into that tent." Tariq pointed at the tent that Deja had seen the other hostages go into. "There is food and water in there. You must stay there until the sandstorm has stopped."

"Um, okay." Deja nodded. He smiled at her and then walked off. He joined some of the men in taking the horses into a tent. They were really prepared for everything, Deja thought to herself. They had horses, jeeps and a large campsite. She quickly headed over to the tent and joined the other hostages.

Chapter 3

Aaron stretched his arms as he stepped out of his tent the next morning. It had been about an hour since the sandstorm had stopped. He slipped his hands in his pockets and drew a deep breath of fresh air. He always enjoyed taking a stroll in the morning because the air was nice and fresh.

Aaron turned his head when he heard sand crunching beneath someone's shoes, and he saw one of the hostages. It was the woman who had asked him if he was there to kill them. She was about five feet and six inches tall. She had fair skin and curly brown hair. She walked up to him and stood beside him.

"The sandstorm has finally stopped," she said. "It was so weird hearing the sand crushing against the tent. I've never witnessed a sandstorm before."

"I see," Aaron replied.

"What time is it?"

Aaron glanced at his watch. "5:30," he replied.

"Wow, it's so early." The woman looked up and drew a long breath. "The air is nice," she added. Aaron did not respond. He had been having a quiet, peaceful moment until she came out. Her talking was ruining his peace.

She turned to face him. "Are you a policeman?" she asked him.

"No," he replied.

"A soldier? Or Al-Nurat's version of the FBI?"

Aaron slowly turned his head and looked at her. She was staring at him with a face full of curiosity. "Neither," he replied. She crossed her eyebrows.

"Then what?"

"You ask a lot of questions."

"You and your men came to rescue us from the nomads. We don't know who you are or where you will be taking us. It's natural for me to have questions." She placed her hands on her hips.

"We work with the government." Aaron was not going to reveal his identity to her. He barely knew her, and he was sure that he was not going to meet her again. There was no reason for him to divulge anything about himself to her. She just needed to know that he was there to help her.

"Like the CIA then?" she asked. Aaron sighed.

"Something like that." He hoped that she would go away after that.

"I just wanted to tour the desert. Actually, I didn't want to. A friend thought I was not adventurous enough, and so she dared me." She laughed sardonically. "Who knew that a simple tour would turn out like this? I will never come back into the desert."

Aaron sympathized with her but she talked too much. It was far too early in the morning for that. "Why don't you go back into your tent and rest a little longer?" he asked.

"I'm okay. I'll rest when I get back to the city. It's hard for me to sleep in the same room as people I barely know," she replied. "The noise from the sandstorm didn't help either."

"You talk too much," Aaron spat out. He had thought if he answered a few of her questions, she would be satisfied and return to the tent. However, that didn't seem to be the case. She just kept going on and on.

She gasped and looked at him. "I just had this weird situation happen to me. I could have been killed! Is it wrong for me to talk to you about it?" she spat out. She was not pleased with him. Her tone and facial expression made it obvious to him.

"But you were not killed," he said.

"Whatever." She turned on her heel and walked off. Aaron watched her head back to the tent. She stopped walking and looked at him. "Jerk," she said. Aaron raised his eyebrows. She looked away and kept walking back to the tent. He couldn't understand why she was so angry. He had only been honest with her. Aaron just shrugged his shoulders and slipped his hands into his pocket.

"Did she just call you a jerk?" Tariq asked as he approached Aaron.

"Yes," Aaron replied.

"Why?"

"I don't know." Aaron shrugged his shoulders.

"Were you speaking to each other?" Tariq asked. Aaron shook his head. "She couldn't have randomly called you a jerk."

"She was the one talking, and she did a lot of that."

Tariq laughed a little. "That did not sit well with you," he said.

"I told her that she talked too much."

Tariq snickered and shook his head. "That explains why she was offended. You cannot say that to a woman," he said. Aaron rolled his eyes. He never understood why women were so sensitive.

"I am just glad that we have finally caught these nomads," said Aaron

"Me too," Tariq replied.

"When we get back to the capital, hand them over to the police. If they had done their job correctly, we wouldn't have had to step in." Aaron and Tariq had worked together for a long time and were good friends. For months, they had been concerned about the nomads kidnapping people. They had waited for the police to arrest them but the police hadn't been successful.

"Your father is just as disappointed with the police as you are. He will probably fire a lot of people," Tariq replied.

"As he should." Aaron turned on his heel. "Now that the sandstorm has passed, we need to leave as soon as possible," he added as he walked away.

***

The drive back to the city took just about an hour. Aaron along with some of his men returned to the city with the hostages. Tariq and the rest of the men took the nomads to the police.

"Mina," Aaron called one of his men. "I need you to deal with the hostages. Either give them money or provide transport for them."

"I will do." Mina bowed his head to Aaron.

"Good." Just as Aaron was about to walk off, he was approached by the curly-haired woman.

"Thank you for bringing us back to the capital," she said to him.

"It's fine," he replied to her.

"Earlier, I didn't know whether or not I could trust you." She sighed. "Anyw—"

Before she could finish speaking, Aaron cut her off. "If you need money or transport, speak to him." He pointed at Mina and then walked off. He had other matters to attend to. He didn't want to end up listening to her talking so much again.

Chapter 4

"I was still talking!" Deja called out after him but he kept on walking. She stood there and watched him walk away. He had cut her off and just walked away. She shook her head and turned her attention away from him. She placed her hands on her hips and looked around. They had parked in a parking lot outside a shopping mall. It was good to be back in the capital city. Back to safety.

Deja looked at the man who was giving the hostages money. He smiled at her. "Would you like to be escorted to your destination or would you like money for transport?" he asked her.

"Just some cab fare, please," she replied. He gave her a few Al Nurat dollars for the cab. Deja thanked him and went on her way. There was a taxi stand across the street. She quickly made her way over and jumped into one of the taxis. She gave the driver the address of the place she was staying at, and they were off within seconds.

Deja arrived at the apartment almost twenty minutes later. She opened the front door and walked in. She had only stayed there for two days before she went to tour the desert but it felt like home. She was just happy to be out of the desert. If it weren't for the men in blue, things could have been bad for her and the other hostages.

Suddenly the front door opened and in walked Kara, her best friend. "Deja, I'm here!" she cried out cheerfully. Deja had to fly out to Al Nurat without Kara because Kara had been at a family wedding. Deja was glad that Kara had finally arrived. She had so much to tell her.

"This is a nice apartment," said Kara as she put her suitcase down on the wooden floor. She dangled the house keys with a big smile on her face. "I just collected my keys at the reception. This is so exciting." She giggled a little. Deja had felt the same way when she had arrived at the apartment.

"I was kidnapped," Deja blurted out. She couldn't share the excitement with Kara. She needed to tell her what had happened in the desert.

"I'm sorry, what?" Kara crossed her eyebrows.

"Yeah." Deja ran her hand through her curls. Kara let out a laugh.

"You're not making sense. Are you trying to play a joke on me or something?" Kara asked. She took her handbag and put it down on the glass table in the middle of the living room.

"I went to tour the desert like you suggested," said Deja.

"Yeah, how did that go?" Kara smiled and crossed her arms over her chest.

"And we got attacked by nomads."

"What?"

"Yeah." Deja sat down on the sofa and told Kara everything that had happened in the desert. Kara just stood there with her jaw hanging open.

"All this happened since the last time we spoke?" she asked. Deja nodded. "This is crazy."

"Tell me about it," Deja replied. She too was still in shock about the entire thing. It was as if it was a dream.

"Did they hurt you?" Kara asked. Deja shook her head.

"Thankfully, they didn't," she said. She rose to her feet. "Now that I am safe, and you are here, let's go out and do something," she said.

"I feel bad for daring you to tour the desert," Kara replied. Deja shrugged her shoulders.

"Then you can pay for dinner." Deja wiggled her eyebrows mischievously. Kara laughed.

"Of course."

Deja walked over to Kara and linked her arm into Kara's. "Don't beat yourself up, I took the dare.

Besides, it's not like you knew about the nomads," Deja reassured Kara.

"Let's go have some fun before we start work." Kara picked up her handbag from the table. The two of them headed for the front door.

***

Beep! Beep! The alarm sounded so loudly, it woke Deja up with a fright. She quickly pressed the snooze button. She groaned as she rolled out of bed. She headed to the bathroom for a quick shower. As Deja was taking a shower, she couldn't help but wonder what her first day at Beshara Oils was going to be like. She was definitely keen to start working but she was also nervous about working in a different country.

Deja got out of the shower and headed back to her bedroom. She towel-dried herself and then slipped into a navy-blue dress. Since she was in a Middle Eastern country, she knew it was not a good idea to wear clothes that were too revealing. So, she made sure to wear a loose-fitting dress that came below the knee and low heels.

After she was finished getting dressed, Deja headed to the kitchen for some breakfast. Kara was already in the kitchen setting up the breakfast table. "Morning," Kara greeted Deja cheerfully.

"I don't know where you get so much energy in the morning." Deja said as she walked into the kitchen. She pulled out a chair for herself and sat down.

"I don't know why you are so grumpy every morning." Kara joined Deja at the table. Deja picked up a fork and started eating the scrambled eggs.

"Any time before 10 a.m. is too early to function."

Kara laughed and shook her head. The two of them ate their breakfast and then headed off to work. Deja and Kara were going to be working at the same company. Deja was grateful for that. Beshara Oils had recruited Kara and Deja from MIT while they were in their final year of engineering studies.

They arrived at Beshara Oils fifteen minutes early. They had to give their names to the security guard at the gate before they could get in. They walked through the gate and approached the massive building. The automatic glass doors slid open and they walked into the building. Deja was impressed by how beautiful and sophisticated the place was.

"Good morning," the receptionist greeted them cheerfully.

"Morning," Deja and Kara chorused.

"Welcome to Beshara Oils." She was very perky and bubbly.

"Thank you," they both replied.

"Follow me, I will show you to the conference room," said the receptionist as she started walking towards the elevator. Deja was aware that the first thing on the agenda was a meeting because she had received an e-mail letting her know about it. The new hires were required to attend a short meeting with their managers. The meeting was going to highlight what was required of them.

Kara and Deja followed the receptionist into the elevator. They went all the way up to the tenth floor. The perky receptionist showed them into the conference room and then returned downstairs. Kara and Deja were the first ones in the conference room.

"We are the first ones here," Kara pointed out.

"Thankfully," said Deja as she pulled out one of the black leather chairs. She sat down in the chair facing the door. She never liked having her back to the entrance. Kara sat down next to her. Deja looked around while they waited. The conference room was quite big. There was a long, oval wooden table in the middle of the room. There were black leather chairs around the table. The room had large windows.

Moments later, the receptionist walked in with three guys dressed smartly. They were new hires also. They introduced themselves as Omar, Fadi and Basil. Deja wondered how many new hires there were going to be. At 9 a.m. sharp, a man dressed in a pair of black trousers and a pink shirt walked in.

"Good morning," he said with a smile. "I am Mr. Tadros. I will be your manager and your first point of contact." He sat down at the table, welcomed them to the company and started talking about their roles. They were the newest engineers at the company and were going to be working under Mr. Tadros. They were a small team that he was going to manage. He glanced at his watch.

"The sheikh will be here soon," he said. Deja and Kara looked at each other.

"Sheikh Beshara?" Basil asked. Mr. Tadros nodded.

"You are all lucky enough to meet the sheikh on your first day." Mr. Tadros grinned. Deja wondered why they were lucky.

"Does the sheikh work here all the time?" Omar asked.

"No, obviously he has many matters all over the country that he needs to attend to. So, you will not see him around a lot."

"It'll be nice meeting the sheikh," said Fadi.

"Before you all meet the sheikh, it is important that you know a few things about him. The sheikh is very stern. Make sure you're well-behaved at all times, and that you address him respectfully."

Suddenly the door swung open and in walked a tall man dressed in a navy-blue suit and a crisp white shirt. The suit complemented his muscular figure. He was looking at his phone. Mr. Tadros and the other guys rose from their seats.

"Good morning, sheikh," said Mr. Tadros as he bowed his head. Kara and Deja quickly rose to their feet also. Deja stared at the man in disbelief. She couldn't believe that he was the sheikh. She recognized him. He was the rude man from the tent, the one she had met in the desert.

Chapter 5

"Morning," the sheikh answered Mr. Tadros. He approached the head of the table and sat down. They all sat down after the sheikh was seated.

"These are the new hires," said Mr. Tadros. The sheikh looked up from his phone and scanned the room. He stopped when he made eye contact with Deja. He slightly raised his eyebrows. Deja had a feeling that he was surprised to see her. In that case, the feeling was mutual. She was surprised to see him. Deja had thought that she was never going to see him again. "I am sure that you are all already aware that the sheikh's family owns this company. So, he's your boss," Mr. Tadros added with a grin.

Deja's eyes slightly widened. The sheikh's family owned the company. Deja wanted to scream at the top of her lungs. That just made things that much more awkward between them.

"Introduce yourselves," said the sheikh.

"My name is Omar," Omar quickly introduced himself to the sheikh. Basil, Kara and Fadi then introduced themselves. Deja waited until everyone else had introduced themselves. She felt awkward. When she had met the sheikh, he hadn't been that warm towards her. He told her that she talked too much.

"My name is Deja. Like Kara, I was also recruited from MIT," she said. The sheikh was looking at her as she spoke. It was as if he had been waiting to hear her speak, to find out what her name was and where she was from.

"You're from MIT?" he asked. She was the only one he had responded to.

"Yes sir," she replied. The tension was so thick you could almost cut it with a knife.

After the introductions, Mr. Tadros started talking about the agenda for the rest of the day. Deja could barely concentrate on what he was saying. There were so many things running through her mind. She wondered what the sheikh was thinking about her. She wondered if they were going to run into each other often. Her subconscious convinced her that since he was a sheikh and his family owned the company, they were probably not going to run into each other often nor were they going to work with each other.

"I have another meeting to get to," the sheikh said as he rose to his feet. Mr. Tadros and the guys quickly rose to their feet. Kara and Deja stood up after they saw the others stand up. They were the only

Americans in the room. They were not used to the Al Nurat ways.

"Thank you for coming, sheikh." Mr. Tadros bowed his head and so did Fadi, Omar and Basil. Kara and Deja looked at each other with similar facial expressions. Deja was wondering why they were bowing their heads to the sheikh. Kara was probably wondering the same thing.

"The sheikh is amazing in person," said Omar. He seemed like such a big fan of the sheikh.

"He is," said Mr. Tadros. "Follow me, I will show you around."

As they were heading out of the room, Deja squeezed Kara's hand tightly. "Oh my lord," she whispered.

"What's wrong?" Kara whispered back.

"The sheikh."

"Yes, he is very handsome."

Deja turned her head and looked at Kara. "That's not what I was going to say," she whispered.

"Then what?" Kara asked.

"He is the man from the tent."

"What?" Kara said loudly. Mr. Tadros turned and looked at them.

"Is everything okay?" he asked. Kara cleared her throat and smiled.

"Yes sir," she replied. "This place is incredible," she added. Mr. Tadros slipped his hands in his pockets.

"This place was renovated last year. The Besharas spent a lot of money of making this place look as good as it does."

Deja agreed with Kara. The place really did look good. They all walked to a room opposite the elevators. Inside were a few L-shaped tables. Each desk had a computer and a printer on it. The floors were made of expensive wood. On the right side of the room, there was a cute little kitchen. There was a water dispenser, coffee machines, a fridge, a sink, a microwave and a table in the kitchen. Everything just looked so expensive and clean.

"This is your office. Pick a table," said Mr. Tadros. Deja and Kara looked at each other excitedly. They quickly rushed over to the desks on the left side of the room. They were by the windows and next to each other.

The rest of the day progressed smoothly. Deja was grateful for that. She had been slightly worried about what her first day was going to be like. Despite the surprise in the conference room, her day had gone well.

"Finally work is over," Kara said to Deja as they walked out of the building.

"Why finally? I didn't think the day dragged," Deja replied.

"The day was fine but I've been dying to talk about the sheikh."

"Oh my God." Deja burst into laughter. She had been dying to talk about him also. "Kara, I still can't believe it."

"Neither can I. You forgot to mention how attractive he is."

Deja rolled her eyes. "When I told you about him, I focused on the fact that he had come to rescue us," she said.

"And on how rude he had been to you."

"Yeah, the last time I saw him, he just cut me off and said what he wanted to say and then walked off." Deja shook her head. "Well, it's not like we argued or anything. I shouldn't feel awkward about this," she added. Kara pulled her phone out of her handbag.

"The one thing I don't understand is why they were bowing to him," she said.

"I know! That was odd," Deja replied. "Maybe it's the culture. He is a sheikh after all."

The security guard opened the gate for them as they approached. Deja noticed that Kara was suddenly walking slowly. She turned around and looked at her. Kara was texting.

"What are you doing?" Deja asked her.

"I am searching for Sheikh Beshara on Google," she replied.

"Why?"

"Because we know nothing about him. We are going to be working for this man, so it makes sense that we research him." Kara grinned at Deja.

"Yeah, okay." Deja let out a laugh.

"No way!" Kara spat out.

"What, Kara? What is it?" Deja stopped walking and looked at Kara.

"This is your sheikh." She showed Deja the screen.

"I know what he looks like." Deja was confused as to why Kara was showing her a picture of the sheikh. "He looks sharp though," Deja pointed out. The sheikh was dressed in a cream-colored suit that complemented his body. He had one hand in his pocket and the other was down at his side. His beard made his stare even more intense.

"Read the caption below!" Kara spat out.

"Oh." Deja lowered her gaze and read the caption below the picture. She gasped loudly and looked at Kara. "No way!" she said.

"Apparently!"

"That explains why Mr. Tadros was bowing his head to him," said Deja. Of course they would bow their heads to the sheikh since he was the crown prince of Al Nurat.

Chapter 6

The maids bowed their heads to Aaron as he walked into the dining room. He approached the table and bowed his head to his father. He kissed his mother on the cheek. She smiled and rubbed his cheek. Aaron pulled out his chair and joined his parents at the dining table.

"You went into the office today?" his father asked him.

"Yes, I did," he replied. The maids dished out the food for them. Aaron picked up his fork and started eating.

"Did you meet the two girls from MIT?" The king took a sip of his drink. Every year, Beshara Oils recruited graduates from MIT. The king was always interested in new talent.

"Briefly," Aaron replied. He was still shocked about meeting Deja. That was her name; Deja. She was the woman he had met in the desert, and now she was working at his company. It was the weirdest coincidence.

"One of them supposedly achieved very high grades. I am particularly interested to see what she can do."

"Which one is that?"

"I cannot remember her name. It was a rather odd name." The king chewed on his meat. "Deshia or Degia," he added.

"Deja," Aaron said softly.

"That was it." The king laughed a little. "It is a rather peculiar name."

"How smart is she?" the queen asked.

"She has graduated at the top of her class," said the king. Aaron raised an eyebrow. He hadn't expected her to be such an intelligent person. He only thought of her as talkative.

"Wow."

The king looked at Aaron. "Your birthday is coming up soon," he said.

"Yes, and we are going to have an extravagant celebration," said the queen.

"Mother, I do not wish to have a party," said Aaron. He didn't want to make a big deal out of his birthday. He never wanted to. Unfortunately for him, his mother always made a big deal out of his birthdays. She hosted very expensive and elaborate parties. She would invite a lot of people.

"That is nonsense," said the queen. "It is your thirtieth. It is a big deal."

Aaron shrugged his shoulders. "A quiet affair would be much more appropriate."

"For who?"

"For myself."

The queen dismissed him with her hand. "This is also a great opportunity for you to meet a beautiful young lady," she said.

"Oh lord," Aaron mumbled.

"I will invite princesses from other countries, daughters of sheikhs and ministers. You will have your pick."

The king laughed a little. He looked at his wife. "Is this your attempt to entice him?" he asked her.

"Yes. By now he should have been married anyway," she said to him.

"I am just not ready for marriage," said Aaron.

"That has been your excuse for the past few years. Now that you are turning thirty, I will not let you get away with it any longer."

Aaron couldn't picture his life as a husband. The whole idea of marriage didn't interest him too much. His mother always told him that his life wouldn't change after marriage. He would still be able to do whatever he wanted. The only difference was that he would have a woman by his side. Aaron didn't think that way. He knew that if he had a wife, she would want his attention. She would want him to love her and be romantic. Aaron was not a romantic man and he didn't believe in love.

***

The next morning, Aaron went to work. The receptionist greeted him cheerfully as usual. Aaron wondered how someone could be that happy all the time. He walked into the elevator and pressed the button for the tenth floor. He pulled out his phone and started reading an email.

When the elevator doors opened, Aaron looked up from his phone and immediately made eye contact with Deja. She was sitting at her desk in the office opposite the elevators. Her curly hair was tied up into a high bun. She wore silver stud earrings. She looked surprised to see him. She quickly looked away. Aaron walked out of the elevator and took a left. He walked down the hall and headed to his office.

"Good morning, sheikh," Rania greeted Aaron as he approached her desk. Rania was his secretary.

"Hi Rania, can you get the files on the new hires?" he replied.

"Yes, sheikh."

Aaron walked past her desk and opened his office door. He walked into the office and sat down on his tufted white leather chair. Rania walked in moments later with a small pile of files. She put them on his glass desk and then walked out. Aaron looked through the pile for Deja's file.

He pulled out her file from the pile and opened it. She was twenty-four years old. Young, he thought to himself. Just like his father had said, she had graduated at the top of her class. He read through her transcript, she had impressive grades. Other than academic information, there was a basic background check. Beshara Oils ran background checks on all its employees before they started work.

Deja had no criminal record and had a decent credit score. There was no more information. Aaron wasn't sure what he was looking for but he felt unsatisfied. It was as if he wanted to know more about her. He closed her file and put it back on the pile. He leaned back into his chair and stroked his chin with his finger.

There was a knock on the door. "Come in," Aaron called out. The door slowly opened and in walked Deja. Aaron raised an eyebrow.

"Um." She cleared her throat. "Sheikh." She bowed her head awkwardly. She wore a calf-length grey dress. It wasn't tight-fitting but it complemented her curvy figure. She wore a pair of black high heels.

"Deja," he said.

"You know my name?"

"You told me yesterday."

"Oh yeah." She looked slightly embarrassed. She held tightly onto the document in her hand.

"What brings you to my office?" Aaron wondered why she was in his office. He wondered if she wanted to talk about the desert. Either way, he was intrigued. He leaned back into his chair and waited for her response.

"Mr. Tadros sent me over with this document for you to sign," she said. She approached his desk and put it down.

"I thought you were here to apologize to me," he said. Deja raised her eyebrows.

"For what?" she asked him.

"Calling me a jerk."

Deja cleared her throat. "It was warranted," she said. Aaron stared at her for a moment. Then he picked up the document and started reading it. He picked up his fountain pen and signed it.

"How?" he asked her.

"Excuse me?" Deja replied.

"How was calling me a jerk warranted?"

"You were rather cold to me." She bowed her head and retrieved the document from his desk. She turned on her heel and bumped into Tariq who was walking into Aaron's office. "Oh my God!" she spat out.

"Wait, have I seen you before?" he said to her.

"Apparently it's a very small world," she said to him. Tariq laughed.

"What are you doing here?"

"I started working here yesterday."

Tariq raised his eyebrows. "Really?" he asked. Deja nodded.

"Do you work here?" she asked.

"Yes." Tariq smiled.

"Ah, well it's good to see you again." Deja headed for the door and walked out. Tariq looked at Aaron. He looked rather amused.

"She works here?" Tariq asked Aaron.

"Imagine my surprise when I walked in the conference room and saw her there," Aaron replied. Tariq laughed.

"It is a small world indeed." Tariq pulled out a chair from Aaron's desk and sat down. Tariq had been friends with Aaron since they were kids because their fathers were friends.

"She is one of the MIT graduates," said Aaron. Tariq's eyes widened.

"Really?" he asked. He let out a laugh. "Well, that is interesting," he added.

Chapter 7

Deja walked over to her desk and then sat down. Kara rolled in her chair over to Deja. "How did it go?" she asked her.

"It was freaking awkward," Deja replied. Kara laughed.

"I bet it was. What happened?"

"I made a fool out of myself."

"How?"

"I said sheikh and bowed my head to him. He then said Deja. I said you know my name? And he said you gave it to me yesterday," said Deja. She cringed just remembering it. She had forgotten about introducing herself to him yesterday.

"Deja!" Kara burst into laughter. "Then what happened?" she asked.

"He asked me if I was there to apologize for calling him a jerk."

Kara's eyes widened. "Oh no," she said.

"Yup, he remembered. When I called him a jerk, he didn't even respond. He just stood there looking at me. I didn't think he cared." Deja sighed. She was suddenly not sure if things were going to progress smoothly for her at Beshara Oils.

"Well, did you apologize?" Kara asked.

"No."

"Deja!"

"I told him that it was warranted."

Kara's eyes widened so much it was as if they were going to pop out of her head. "Do you want to lose your job or something?" she asked her.

"It just came out," Deja replied. She was regretting it. She wished that she had just apologized to him.

"Oh honey." Kara laughed a little. "Did he look angry after you said that?"

"No."

Basil approached Deja and Kara. "It's time to go," he said to them. Kara and Deja nodded their heads and rose to their feet. Mr. Tadros was taking them to see the company's oil rigs.

***

There was so much fuss in the office on Friday. From her desk facing the elevators, Deja could see people running back and forth, and coming and going. She wondered what was happening.

Suddenly the elevator doors opened and a tall man dressed in a charcoal grey suit walked out. His hair had a few greys in it. He had broad shoulders and a large body frame. He looked somewhat intimidating. He walked out of the elevator and took a left turn. He had a few men with him.

"The king!" Fadi cried out. Deja whipped her head in his direction.

"What?" she asked him.

"That was the king," he replied.

"The king is here?" Basil asked.

"Yes, He just came out of the elevator," Fadi replied. Deja rolled her chair over to Kara's desk.

"Did you see him?" she asked Kara.

"No, damnit. I wish I did," she replied.

"I did. I was staring at him and wondering who he was," Deja said.

"What does he look like?"

"Stern, intimidating, tall."

"Does he look like your sheikh?"

Deja crossed her eyebrows. That was the second time that Kara had referred to Aaron as her sheikh. "He is not my sheikh," she said.

"Well, if you don't want him, I'll take him," said Kara. Deja frowned. "He is handsome and has a great body."

Deja shook her head. "No way."

"Hmph." Kara smiled at Deja. Mr. Tadros walked into the office and walked over to Deja and Kara.

"Deja, come with me please," he said to her. Deja rose from her seat.

"Is everything okay?" she asked him.

"I have no clue."

Deja looked at Kara. Kara shrugged her shoulders. Deja straightened her black dress and followed Mr. Tadros out of the office. They took a right turn and walked down the hall. Deja noticed that they were going to Aaron's office. Her stomach immediately knotted up. Was he firing her for calling him a jerk and not being apologetic about it?

Mr. Tadros knocked on the sheikh's office door before he walked in. Deja raised her eyebrows when she walked in and saw Aaron and the king sitting at the sofas in Aaron's office.

"Deja is here, your highness," he said.

"You may leave," the king dismissed him. Mr. Tadros bowed his head before he left. Deja stood by the door with her fingers laced together. The king gestured for her to come closer. Deja walked over and bowed her head to him.

"You wished to see me?" she asked.

"Have a seat," he said. Aaron stared at her with a blank expression. He kept his gaze on her as she sat down.

"Thank you," Deja said to the king. Now that she was close to him, she could see that Aaron looked so much like his father. They even had similar voices. The king's voice was just huskier and deeper than Aaron's.

"I came to the office because I had some matters to attend to. While I was here, I thought I should meet you."

"Me? Why?"

The king laughed softly. "Don't panic. It's nothing bad," he said.

"I don't understand why you would want to see me." She looked at Aaron for answers but he just shrugged his shoulders.

"I have heard good things about you," said the king.

"You have?" Who would have said good things about her to the king? Deja wondered. She had only been working at Beshara Oils for a week.

"I heard that you graduated at the top of your class," he said.

"Yes, I did," Deja replied.

"Very impressive."

"Thank you, it was not easy."

"I can imagine." The king picked up a porcelain cup and took a sip. Deja had been so nervous that she hadn't even noticed that there was a cup on the table. She hadn't noticed much; only Aaron and his father. "I also had a look at your thesis," he added.

"You read my thesis?" Deja spat out. That was quite surprising to her.

"Not the entire thing but I was impressed by what I read."

"Thank you." Deja was feeling nervous and confused. Just what was going on? Why had the king asked to see her?

"I can see you are an intelligent young lady and I would like to make good use of your brains."

"You would?"

The king nodded. Aaron looked at his father. "You have met my son?" The king gestured towards Aaron.

"Yes, I have," she said.

"Good," he replied. Deja was wondering why that was good. "He is about to start working on a new project. I think it would be a fantastic idea if you could work on it with him." Aaron raised his eyebrows.

"Father," he said.

"It is a good idea," the king said to Aaron. "This way, you can get to see what she is capable of. Then you can make the decision whether she is a good fit for the company."

Great! Deja thought to herself. The man she had called a jerk had her future in his hands. It made her extremely nervous. She really wanted to do well at Beshara Oils. It was one of the biggest oil companies in the world and they had handpicked her from MIT. She really wished that she had apologized to Aaron when she had a chance.

"She is a recent graduate. She doesn't have much experience yet," said Aaron.

"Then you can be her mentor," said the king. He looked at Deja and smiled. "What do you think, Miss Gibson?"

Deja forced a smile. "It's a great opportunity but it makes me feel nervous. Like the sheikh says, I don't have experience," she said. The king smiled.

"Will you work with my son?"

Aaron turned and looked at Deja. He looked like he was anticipating her answer. Deja smiled. "Yes, I will work with your son and I will do my best," she said.

"Good." The king rose to his feet. Deja and Aaron also stood up. "I must return to the palace now," he said. Deja bowed her head to him. He walked out of the office; leaving Aaron and Deja alone.

The Sheikh's Choice

"So, you're my mentor now," Deja said to Aaron.

Chapter 8

"Great," Aaron replied as he walked over to his desk. He didn't seem too pleased about the entire thing. Deja felt awkward about having to work with Aaron but it didn't seem as though she had a choice. The king had personally assigned her to work with his son. It was a big deal and Deja was both excited and nervous.

"What kind of project will we be working on?" Deja asked Aaron.

"I will let you know soon," Aaron replied without looking at her. He just focused on the documents he was reading. Deja watched him pen his signature on the paper.

"Okay but you know—" Before Deja was finished speaking, Aaron cut her off.

"You may leave," he said to her and dismissed her with his hand. Deja widened her eyes and gasped. She wanted to talk to Aaron about this project the king wanted them to work on but Aaron wasn't interested. She wished he hadn't dismissed her so rudely. Deja just turned on her heel and headed for the exit. She walked out of his office and had a thought to leave his door open just to be petty because he was rude to her. However, she knew that she had to tread carefully since he could fire her if he wanted.

Kara jerked her head up when Deja walked back into the office. She looked a bit worried. "Why did he call you out?" Kara asked her.

"You will not believe what just happened," Deja replied. She still couldn't believe it either.

"Deja, a word?" Mr. Tadros called out. Deja turned around and found him standing in the doorway of the office.

"Okay." She quickly walked over to him. He took a few steps back and gestured for Deja to come closer. Deja cautiously followed him. She wondered what he wanted to talk to her about outside the office.

"What did the king say to you?" Mr. Tadros asked her.

"Ah, the king," she said. It was natural that he would be curious. It was the king after all. "He asked me to work on a project with Sheikh Beshara," she told him.

"What?" Mr. Tadros spat out. "No, he didn't." He laughed a little.

"Yes, he did." Deja shrugged her shoulders. "I'm still trying to wrap my head around it."

Mr. Tadros shook his head. "That doesn't make any sense. Why would he ask you, a new hire to work with Sheikh Beshara?" he asked. He was looking at Deja as though she was crazy.

"He seems to know of my progress when I was at MIT."

Mr. Tadros snapped his fingers. "Ah! He must have been impressed and he wanted to put a face to the name," he said.

"Something like that."

"Now that you have caught the king's attention, you must work hard and make our team look good." He tapped her on the shoulder and walked back towards the office. Deja sighed and shrugged her shoulders. Mr. Tadros didn't believe that the king wanted her to work with Aaron. She was doubtful about it. Maybe Aaron was going to refuse to work with her.

Deja slowly walked back into their office. Kara was looking at her with so much curiosity in her face. "I'll tell you later," Deja mouthed to her. Kara nodded. Deja pulled out her chair from her desk and sat down. She looked at the files on her desk and just sighed. Earlier, they each had been given files with information on some of the company's wells. They were to review the procedures and everything else involved in oil production.

***

"Ah, home-time." Kara stretched her arms. "All that reading was making me fall asleep."

"Tell me about it," Deja replied as they walked out of the main building.

"Oh! Sheikh Beshara," Kara pointed out. Deja turned her head and saw the sheikh getting into an expensive-looking car. Deja gasped.

"That's right, I still have to tell you what happened earlier."

"Tell me."

"When Mr. Tadros came to call for me, he escorted me to the sheikh's office."

"Why?"

"The king was looking for me."

"Why was the king looking for you?" Kara spat out. She stopped walking and stared at Deja with her eyes widened. Deja also stopped walking and turned to face Kara.

"Apparently he was impressed with my academic achievements."

"He was?" Kara gasped. "Well, you did graduate at the top of our class." She nudged Deja playfully. Deja smiled.

"He wants me to work on a project with his son," she added. Kara's green eyes almost popped out of their sockets.

"What? No way!!" she spat out. Deja nodded.

"I was just as shocked as you are," Deja replied.

"That's incredible." Kara leaped with excitement. "This is a great opportunity for you. It's important that you do your best," she added.

Deja shook her head. "I have mixed emotions about this." She shrugged her shoulders and started walking. Kara also started walking.

"Why? The only feelings you should be experiencing are those of happiness," she said.

"First of all, I am not even sure if the sheikh wants to work with me. He didn't seem pleased about it and when I tried to talk to him about it, he just cut me off and dismissed me from his office."

"He did?" Kara asked. Deja nodded. "Let's hope that he doesn't refuse to work on the project with you or put you on another one. Anyway, it was the king's order so I am sure he has to oblige."

Deja shrugged her shoulders. "The other thing is that people will think that it's unfair that I've only been working here for less than a week and I already get to work with the sheikh," she said.

"Yeah, people will talk about you and will try to discourage you. They will be jealous. That's why you've got to do a good job."

"I know." Deja crossed her arms over her chest. "I just wish that I had been working here a little bit longer and had done well on a project," she added. She felt as though she was getting an opportunity she hadn't worked hard for.

"Deja! Snap out of it," Kara spat out.

"What?" Deja raised her eyebrows.

"The king gave you this opportunity because of your past achievements. It's not like you don't deserve this."

"Look!" Deja pointed at Aaron's car driving past them. "He couldn't even offer us a lift," she said.

"Did you think he would?"

"No." Deja laughed a little. "It's going to be so awkward working with him."

"That's why you should apologize for calling him a jerk." Kara's reply was followed by a cheeky laugh.

"I thought about apologizing when Mr. Tadros sent me to his office but the words didn't come out. Now it's just too late."

"You'll just have to be on your best behavior and basically do everything he says."

"So, kiss up to him?"

"I wouldn't mind." Kara giggled. Deja smiled and shook her head.

"He's not that attractive," Deja said.

"You're either blind or lying to yourself."

Deja burst into laughter. "Neither," she replied.

Chapter 9

Aaron was sitting at his desk when a knock sounded against the door. "Come in," he called out. Mr. Tadros walked into his office and shut the door behind him.

"Good morning, sheikh," he said as he bowed his head to Aaron.

"Morning," Aaron replied.

"You wanted to see me?"

Aaron nodded as he leaned back in his seat. "As you know, I have taken control of the revival of the southern well," he said. The southern well was one of their dried-up wells. It was a big well but one that had dried up so quickly.

"Yes, I am aware," Mr. Tadros replied.

"Deja will be working with me on that project."

"Excuse me?" Mr. Tadros shook his head. "The new girl?"

"Is there another Deja?" Aaron narrowed his gaze

"No, sheikh," Mr. Tadros replied. "I am just shocked that you would work with her. She has only worked here less than a week. We have more seasoned engineers that you could work with," he added.

"I am aware of that," Aaron replied. He really didn't want to work with Deja but then his father had ordered it.

"Sheikh, the others will not like it. There are so many people that have worked here for years and are more deserving of this opportunity."

"Like yourself?"

"Yes, sheikh!" Mr. Tadros spat out. "I have worked here for fifteen years and I have not worked with you on any projects." He looked irritated and upset.

"I understand how you're feeling. However, this is something the king wants. Do you want me to go against his wishes?"

"No, sheikh."

"Good. Release her from her duties when I call for her," said Aaron.

"Yes, sheikh."

"And keep up the good work. Your time for a promotion will come," Aaron knew that Mr. Tadros wanted recognition for his work. It was obvious. However, his work was average. There was nothing about him that made Aaron want to give him a promotion.

"Yes, sheikh," Mr. Tadros replied.

"You may leave."

Mr. Tadros bowed his head to Aaron before he left his office. Aaron sighed as he ran his hand through his hair. He was not particularly keen about working with Deja. She talked too much. Aaron disliked being around people who talked unnecessarily. Aaron rose from his seat and headed to the conference room for a meeting.

As Aaron was heading over to the conference room, he saw Deja in the corridor adjusting her skirt. She wiggled as she pulled down her skirt a little, and then she patted her bottom. Aaron raised his eyebrows. She was well-endowed, and her burgundy skirt made that obvious.

"What are you doing in broad daylight?" Aaron asked Deja as he approached her.

"Huh?" She turned around sharply and faced Aaron. "You startled me," she said.

"That is because you are being obscene."

"I was only adjusting my skirt. It looked a little lopsided." Deja flashed an awkward grin. "Skirts are just awkward. I actually only started wearing skirts when I started working here," she added. Aaron raised an eyebrow. He wondered why she was telling him that. He didn't even bother responding to her. He just slipped his hands in his pockets and walked off.

***

It was just over a week later when Aaron returned from a business trip to Lebanon. His family company was the biggest oil company in the Middle East and supplied oil to many countries in the region. Aaron dropped by the office for a short meeting.

"I will be out of the office for a few hours," Aaron said to his secretary.

"Yes, sheikh," she replied.

"Go and call Deja. Tell her to come to the parking lot."

"Yes, sheikh." The secretary bowed her head to Aaron and then rushed off. Aaron headed out to his car. He waited for Deja in the backseat. She arrived moments later and knocked on his window. Aaron rolled down the window.

"You asked—"

Before she finished speaking, Aaron cut her off. "Get in," he said. Deja raised her eyebrows.

"Huh? Me?"

"Is there anyone else?"

"Um..." Deja scrambled to the other side and got into the car. She sat down next to him and looked at him with a lot of confusion on her face.

"Shut the door then," Aaron said to her.

"Ah, okay." She shut the door.

"Let's go," Aaron said to his driver.

"Yes, sheikh," the driver replied as he started the engine.

"Go where?" Deja asked. She stared at Aaron wide-eyed.

"Relax, I am not kidnapping you."

"That thought never crossed my mind… until now."

Aaron raised an eyebrow and looked at her. He couldn't tell if she was joking or if she was serious. "If we are to work together, it makes sense to visit the well in question," he said.

"Ah." Deja gasped. Her face immediately lit up. "I thought you no longer wanted to work with me," she said.

"Why would you think that?"

"Because I've not heard from you since your father said we should work together."

Aaron narrowed his gaze at her. "It's only been a week," he said. She was so impatient. She must have been dying to work with him; which was understandable. Aaron looked out the window. "Besides, I've been away on business," he added.

"Oh, you were? Where did you go?" she asked.

"It's none of your business."

Aaron heard Deja grunt. He turned his head to look at her. To his surprise, she didn't say anything. She just turned her head and looked out the window. All the times he had spoken to her, she always had something to say and he'd have to cut her off. Aaron was grateful that she was quiet. He had been worried that she would be too talkative during their drive to the southern well.

The quiet didn't last long. Deja started rubbing her back against the seat. "These seats are so comfortable," she said. Deja crossed one leg over the other and giggled. Aaron didn't say anything. He just ignored her.

"Do you ever drive yourself anywhere? Or do you always have a driver?" Deja asked. Aaron sighed and looked at Deja.

"Why are you even asking me that?" he asked her.

"Never mind then." Deja cleared her throat and looked outside. About five minutes later, she turned and looked at Aaron. "I see cars following us," she said.

"My security detail."

"Ah, well that makes sense." Deja just laced her fingers together and looked away.

They arrived at their destination a little while later. "We're here?" Deja asked as the car came to a halt.

"That's why we're stopping," Aaron replied.

"I asked since I've never been here before," Deja mumbled quietly. Aaron heard her and just shook his head. The driver got out of the car and opened the door for Aaron. Deja opened the door for herself and got out of the car.

Aaron slipped a hand in his pocket and started walking towards the oil rig. He was also there to meet with a geologist and a drilling manager. Deja quickly rushed after him. She walked beside him with so much curiosity on her face.

"This is so exciting," she said. "The first oil rig I visited was in Texas. Now I am actually visiting one as a qualified engineer and not a student." She giggled a little. Aaron didn't respond. He just shook his head. Her excitement was ridiculous but adorable.

As they were walking, Deja stepped on a stone and stumbled into Aaron. She squeaked as she nearly fell, and grabbed onto his shirt to stop herself from falling. "What the heck!" she complained. Aaron shrugged her hand away.

"Careful," he said to her. He looked at his chest where she had grabbed at him. "You creased my shirt," he said. Deja looked at him with amusement.

"Oh my God," she breathed. "Such a gentleman," she mumbled.

"You might as well speak clearly because I still hear you when you mumble."

"I was falling over. You could have tried to catch me. If I didn't grab onto your shirt, I'd have been on the ground."

"Then you should have been more careful." With that Aaron walked away. He didn't like people suddenly touching him without his permission.

Chapter 10

Deja watched Aaron walking off. All she could do was shake her head. She couldn't believe that after she almost fell over, all he could say to her was that she creased his shirt. He hadn't even tried to catch her. He was such a strange man. Deja sighed and just started walking after him.

Aaron came to a halt when he approached two men. The two men bowed their heads to Aaron. "Good afternoon, sheikh," they said in unison.

"Afternoon, gentlemen," he replied. Aaron stood tall and confident. He was oozing with authority. If Deja hadn't been around him and didn't know how cold and rude he was, she'd have found him attractive. She approached them and stood beside Aaron.

"Hello, my name is Deja," she said to the two men.

"Afternoon," the two men replied.

"Your new secretary?" one man asked. He was the shorter of the two and looked as though he was in his forties.

"No, she is an engineer. She will be working with us on this project," Aaron replied. Both men widened their eyes and looked at Deja.

"Oh, my apologies," the shorter man said to Deja. He looked so shocked; which annoyed Deja a little bit. He had automatically assumed that she was the sheikh's secretary.

"It's fine," Deja replied.

"This is Anwar, he is the drilling manager for this rig. You'll be meeting him a lot in the future," said Aaron. Deja smiled and nodded. "And this is Jacob. He is the geologist you'll be working with also."

"It's nice to meet you both. Let's work well together."

Both men smiled and nodded. They suddenly seemed awkward. They probably felt bad for their assumption. Deja thought it was probably because she was a woman. This meant that she had to work even harder to show them that she was a good engineer. She stood confidently next to Aaron. Somehow him introducing her to the two men made her feel confident.

"This is quite a large well, and we expected more oil from it," Aaron said to Deja. "However, the well dried up quickly. I'd like to try drilling again but using different methods."

"That's quite expensive. If we drill and we don't find anything, it means that we'll lose a lot of money," Deja replied. Drilling for oil was not cheap. The equipment used was very pricey, and a lot of time and money went into drilling.

"You are right. That's why we are going to redo the process of collecting samples and calculations to see if there is any oil."

"Okay." Deja was wondering why they would re-drill a well that had dried up.

"A lot of money was spent on this rig. The initial soil samples we collected were promising. I'd like to re-drill because we need to make a profit from this well. Otherwise we'd have lost a lot of money," Aaron explained. It was if he knew Deja was wondering. She was glad that he explained before she asked.

"Ah." Deja nodded. "It's risky but it'll be worth it if we find a lot of oil."

"Exactly." Aaron turned his attention to Jacob and Anwar. He started telling them about his expectations. He expected the project to not be easy but he expected everyone on board to work hard. Aaron loathed lazy people. He also gave them instructions on what he wanted done next. As he spoke, Deja just watched him. He was quite impressive. He was so manly and regal.

After the meeting with Jacob and Anwar, Deja and Aaron returned to his car. They both got in and sat in the backseat. Deja felt awkward about being in the car with Aaron. Driving up to the rig had been awkward enough. She had attempted to make conversation with him but he hadn't reciprocated at all.

Aaron's driver got into the driver's seat and they were off immediately. "Where are we going now?" Deja asked Aaron.

"Back to the office," he replied. She crossed one leg over the other and looked at Aaron.

"When do we start this project?"

"Now, we just began." Aaron was facing forward as he spoke. Deja noticed that he had very smooth skin with a nice glow.

"What will you need me to do?" she asked him.

"I will let you know soon." Aaron sounded as though he wasn't interested in having a conversation with Deja. She stared at him with a narrowed gaze. If they were going to work together, it would be helpful if he was a bit more forthcoming with information. Deja just sighed heavily. Aaron turned his head and found her staring at him.

Aaron grunted. "You and I will work together to analyze the information the geologist finds and we will think of drilling methods. Our aim is to find as much oil as we can find," he said to her and then looked away.

Deja nodded. "I will do my best to help you," she said. It was going to be her first assignment in the

Beshara company and it made her both excited and nervous. She worried that her lack of experience would show and that the king would be disappointed in her. However, she was not going to voice her concerns to Aaron. It wasn't like he was going to care or listen anyway.

"So, what is it like being the crown prince of Al Nurat?" Deja asked Aaron. She wondered how different his life was to hers. Aaron looked at her and crossed his eyebrows.

"You have so many questions," he replied. His voice was deep and husky as always.

"I don't believe I've asked many questions today."

Aaron raised an eyebrow. "You have." He sighed. "Let's just continue the rest of our journey in silence," he added.

"Yes sir." Deja laced her fingers together and looked outside.

***

They arrived back at the office just after lunch. Aaron and Deja got out of the car and went their separate ways. Deja rushed back up to her office. She greeted Mr. Tadros but he just looked up from his computer with a slight frown on his face.

"Go photocopy those documents," he said to her and pointed at a huge pile on his desk.

"Uh… okay." Deja picked up the files.

"Two copies of each."

"Yes, Mr. Tadros."

As Deja was walking out of the office, she looked at Kara and pouted at her. Kara just smiled. Deja headed over to the photocopier situated at the entrance of the office by the glass doors. She started photocopying the documents, one at a time. There were so many of them.

Deja was almost halfway done when she closed her eyes and rolled her neck from side to side to stretch. When she opened her eyes, she saw Aaron walking out of the elevator. As she watched him walk, she couldn't help but shake her head. How could such a handsome and attractive man be so cold and unfriendly? It wasn't so shocking. It was the same in the USA. The attractive men were usually players.

Aaron turned his head and caught Deja's gaze as he walked past the office. Deja was a little bit startled when Aaron looked at her. His dark gaze made her stomach knot up. She didn't know whether to smile at him or to look away. So, she just stared at him until he was gone.

Chapter 11

Aaron slipped into a pair of beige trousers and a crisp white shirt. He wore brown loafers. He brushed his hair and styled it. His hair had a side part on the left side. The back and sides were shorter than the middle. Aaron finished off his look with silver cufflinks and a silver Rolex. He headed downstairs to the dining room for breakfast.

He normally enjoyed his breakfast in quietness with the morning newspaper. However, today his parents wanted to have breakfast with him. So instead of eating in his private dining room, he went downstairs to the main dining room to join his parents. As Aaron walked into the dining room, the maids all curtsied to him.

"Good morning, Father." Aaron bowed his head to the king, who sat at the head of the table. "Morning, Mother." He kissed her on the cheek. His mother smiled at him warmly.

"Morning, dear," she replied. She was seated at her husband's right. Aaron joined them at the table and sat opposite his mother. The maids quickly served him some food.

"You rarely dine with us these days," said the king.

"Work is keeping me busy," Aaron replied. Aaron had a lot of duties as the eldest son of the Beshara royal family. He had to tend to the family company and he also had princely duties.

"I look forward to hearing good news about the southern well," the king said to Aaron.

"You and I both." Aaron desperately needed to find oil in that well. If he did, it would compensate for all the money that had been spent trying to extract oil from it the first time.

"Let's stop speaking of work," said the queen. She looked at her son. "It is your birthday in two days."

"Oh." Aaron had completely forgotten about his birthday. He wasn't one to celebrate such trivial things. However, his mother always made sure to make a big deal out of it.

A tall, dark and handsome man oozing with arrogance and charm walked into the room.

"Look who's back," he said looking at Aaron with a huge grin on his face. He bowed to the king and kissed the queen on the cheek.

"Joseph." The queen spoke with a warm smile on her face. "You stayed away too long," she protested. Joseph sat down next to the queen.

"Brother, welcome back," said Aaron. His younger brother had been abroad for some time. He liked to travel, party and live life to the fullest.

"You didn't think I would miss your birthday, did you?" Joseph asked Aaron.

"It's just another day of the year."

"Nonsense. You will be turning thirty years old, it is a big deal," said the queen.

"So, there will be a big party then?" Joseph asked.

"Is that all you think about? Parties?" said the king. Aaron and Joseph looked at each other. "When will you grow up? You bring disgrace to the royal family," he added.

"Let's not argue. He only just arrived," said the queen. The king shook his head and rose from the table. Aaron and Joseph also stood up and bowed their heads to the king as he walked out of the room. Joseph sighed as he sat down in his chair.

"Father is not wrong," said Aaron.

"Are you serious right now?" Joseph asked Aaron.

"You are now twenty-seven years old." Aaron sat down. "You can't travel and party forever. It's about time you started to work at the company. It doesn't have to be full-time but you need to do something before father decides to take action," he added.

"I don't want to work at the company. I'm not that interested in oil," Joseph replied.

"But you are interested in the money the company brings."

"You aren't being fair right now."

"I am only advising you as your older brother."

The queen touched Joseph's hand. "I too think you should start working at the company. Otherwise I fear that your father will do something," she said softly. On a few occasions, the king had threatened to stop providing Joseph with any financial support and let him live the life of a commoner. He wanted his son to work at the family company and mature a little bit more.

Joseph rolled his eyes. "I'll come in on Monday and see. If I don't like it then it's not my fault," he said.

"Why Monday? Come in today," said Aaron.

"I just arrived. I am jet-lagged."

Aaron shook his head as he picked up his cup and took a sip of his organic green tea. The queen wiped her mouth with a napkin. "So, about the party on Saturday, there will be plenty of single women," she said.

"Oh really?" Joseph's face lit up.

"Not for you, for Aaron. Now that you are thirty, you definitely have to settle down."

Aaron looked at the expensive Rolex on his wrist. "I have a meeting in twenty minutes," he said and rose from his seat.

"You cannot keep avoiding this subject, Aaron," said his mother.

"Yeah, Aaron. You need a wife," Joseph interjected.

"Stay out of it," Aaron warned. He walked around the table and kissed his mother on the cheek.

"We'll talk when you get back from work," said his mother. Aaron didn't reply. He just walked out of the dining room. He knew that he had to get married sooner or later but he didn't want to rush into it. He didn't even want to talk about it. However, his mother was like a dog with a bone. She was never going to let the matter go.

Aaron arrived at the office just before 9 o'clock. He got out of the car and headed into the building. The chirpy receptionist rose to her feet and bowed her head to Aaron as he walked in.

"Good morning, sheikh," she said with a big smile on her face. Aaron just nodded at her. It was always surprising to him how cheerful she was so early in the morning, and how she stayed that way for the rest of the day. Aaron nodded at her and headed over to the elevator.

"Hold the elevator!" Tariq called out as he ran towards the elevator. Aaron pressed a button and held the doors for him.

"You were coming in today?" Aaron asked Tariq.

"Yes, I have a meeting." Tariq stood beside Aaron in the elevator and pressed the button.

"Ah." Aaron nodded.

"I received an invite from the queen."

"For what?"

"For your birthday party."

"Hmm." Aaron grunted.

"You're not excited?" Tariq asked cheekily. Aaron looked at him with a raised eyebrow. Tariq laughed softly.

"She even mentioned that there will be plenty of single women," said Aaron.

"Nice. I think it's been a while since you've had a dalliance."

"No." Aaron shook his head. "She means to find a wife for me."

"Ah." Tariq nodded. "That's not so bad either. You are of age."

The elevator doors opened. Aaron and Tariq both walked out of the elevator.

"I just hope she finds me a quiet and poised woman," said Aaron. Deja turned a corner and walked towards Aaron and Tariq.

"Good morning, sheikh." She bowed her head to Aaron. She looked at Tariq. "I haven't seen you around for a while," she said to him. Aaron didn't reply to her. He just kept on walking towards his office.

"How are you?" Tariq asked with a smile.

"I'm fine," she replied.

Aaron headed to his office. He walked in and took a seat at his desk. Tariq walked in moments later.

"Hopefully your wife has childbearing hips such as Deja's," said Tariq. Aaron looked at him as though he was strange. "I just noticed how curvy she is," Tariq added before he burst into laughter.

Aaron had noticed a long time ago but he was not going to admit it. "She talks too much," he said.

"Does she?"

Aaron shook his head. "And I have to work with her on the southern well," he said.

"Do you? Why?" Tariq sat down at Aaron's desk.

"It was father's idea. He came in and asked that she and I work together."

"I'm sure it'll be fine."

"It's already annoying. She won't stop asking questions."

There was a knock on the door. "Come in," Aaron called out. Deja walked into the office with a document in her hand.

"Mr. Tadros sent me," she said to him and pointed at the document in her hand.

"Bring it over," he said to her. It was the second time Mr. Tadros had sent Deja to his office with a document. He wondered why he never sent anyone else. Aaron's gaze lowered to her hips as she walked towards him. She wore a black-and-white striped skirt which complemented her wide hips and small waist. Now that Tariq had mentioned her hips, Aaron couldn't help look at them.

Chapter 12

"You may go." Aaron dismissed Deja. Aaron expected her to leave but she didn't leave immediately. She looked as though she had something to say. He was hoping that wasn't the case because she was too talkative for his liking.

Deja cleared her throat. "Will you be calling on me today?" she asked him. Aaron leaned back in his chair and looked at her.

"For what?" he asked.

"To work on the project. Do you have work for me to do? Something to look at?" Her hazel eyes widened. She was a very curious person. Tariq looked at her with so much amusement on his face.

"You are rather impatient," Aaron pointed out.

"I'm sorry, sir, I'm not trying to be impatient. I'm just wondering, so that I can manage my workload."

Aaron raised his eyebrows. He didn't believe her. "I've already told Mr. Tadros that we will be working together. So, he shouldn't be giving you so much to do anyway," he said.

"Ah," Deja replied.

"How is it working here so far?" Tariq asked her.

"It's interesting and exciting."

"You may go." Aaron dismissed her again.

"Okay." Deja nodded. She looked at Tariq. "I'll see you next time," she said to him. She turned on her heel and headed for the door. Aaron watched her walking away. She wasn't bad-looking. She was something like five feet six or seven inches tall. She had an impressive hourglass figure. No doubt she worked hard to stay in shape.

"Aaron," Tariq called out. Aaron turned his head and looked at Tariq. "You're noticing those hips, aren't you?"

"What hips?"

"Deja's childbearing hips."

"No." Aaron was not going to admit that he was looking at her hips. Tariq laughed a little.

"She seems bold, questioning when you're going to call for her."

Aaron shook his head. "When we went to visit the southern well, she basically questioned why I hadn't called for her in a week," he said. Tariq laughed a little.

"She's an interesting woman," said Tariq.

"She just needs to talk less."

Tariq and Aaron talked for   a little while until Tariq had to leave for a meeting. Aaron remained in his office looking over some paperwork. He had new projects to approve, budget proposals to read, completed projects to sign off on; there was always so much for him to do at the office.

***

Deja sighed as she photocopied more documents. Mr. Tadros had taken the rest of the team on a mini field trip to an oil rig. He had asked Deja to stay behind and take care of the filing. Deja was a little bit annoyed about that. She felt as though Mr. Tadros had been treating her differently since he had found out that she was to work on a project with Aaron.

"Miss Gibson?" Deja heard a voice.

"Yes?" she answered as she turned towards the voice. She found Aaron's secretary standing in the doorway of the office.

"The sheikh would like to see you in his office."

"Okay, I'll be there in a moment." Deja quickly took all the documents from the photocopier and placed them neatly on her desk. Then she rushed towards the sheikh's office. She wondered why he was calling on her as she headed to his office. She hoped that he had some work for her. Anything was better than photocopying and filing documents.

Deja straightened her high-waisted grey skirt when she reached the sheikh's office. She gently knocked on the door.

"Come in," Aaron called out. Deja opened the door and slowly walked in.

"You called for me?" she asked.

"Have a seat." Aaron was sitting at his desk. He was wearing a navy-blue shirt and charcoal trousers. No matter what he wore, he always looked good. Deja nodded and walked over to his desk. She pulled out a chair and sat down. There was a white folder on the desk. Aaron pushed it towards Deja.

"What is it?" Deja asked as she picked it up.

"That folder contains information on the southern well. I want you to have a look at it and give me feedback. Let me know if you see anywhere we could improve."

Deja was pleasantly surprised that he had work for her to do. She was even more pleased with the fact that she was finally beginning to do something on the project. "Yes sir," she replied. She flipped the folder open and quickly scanned through the contents.

Deja wanted to ask if she could have the folder for the weekend since it was Friday. She jerked her head up and found him already looking at her. His dark gaze made her nervous. Deja blinked a couple of times before finally asking to take the folder home. Aaron cleared his throat.

"You can take the folder with you and we'll discuss it on Monday," he said to her. Deja wondered if he had been staring at her for a while or they had just looked at each other at the same time.

"Okay, I will do," she replied. Her voice came out smaller than usual. She hoped that Aaron didn't notice. It was just awkward.

"You may go, I have matters to attend to."

Deja nodded. "You must be ready to start your weekend. Of course, you'd have plans."

"Sort of."

"You don't seem enthusiastic about your plans."

"That is because I am not."

"I guess you can choose not to go?"

"I can't not attend an event for which I am the guest of honor."

Deja smiled. "That is true. I suppose you don't have a choice," she said. Aaron sighed as he rose to his feet. Deja also stood up.

"Exactly," he replied.

"Maybe the food will be good?" she said. Aaron raised an eyebrow at her. "You can find a silver lining somewhere."

"And you consider food as a silver lining?"

"Yes." Deja shrugged her shoulders. "Good food can make a horrible event an okay one."

A little, almost non-existent smile tugged at the corner of Aaron's mouth as he shook his head. It was so small and quick that Deja almost missed it. She was shocked. Aaron never smiled or laughed in her presence.

"I have to return to the office. I must finish the filing before the end of my shift," said Deja. Mr. Tadros had instructed her to finish all the photocopying and filing before she went home.

"Sure," Aaron replied. Deja turned on her heel and left Aaron's office. She felt slightly awkward as she walked out. It was the first time that she and Aaron had parted on somewhat good terms. Aaron always cut her off and walked away before Deja was finished speaking, and so she was always annoyed by him.

Chapter 13

Aaron felt bored at his party. There were so many guests and they all wanted to speak to him. He wasn't a social person, he disliked speaking to people he didn't know. However, since he was the crown prince he had to talk to speak to people at such events. There were guests from all over the world at his party. He had to speak to them and thank them for coming.

"Sheikh." Tariq said as he approached Aaron.

"Tariq," Aaron replied. Tariq stood next to Aaron.

"Happy birthday. Are you enjoying your party?"

"Does it look like I am enjoying it?"

"It's your 30th. It is an important milestone in your life. You must enjoy the celebration."

Aaron shrugged his shoulders. Birthdays meant nothing to Aaron. They were just like any other day of the year to him. "It's important to my mother," he said as he looked around the room. The palace ballroom was filled with expensive decorations and ridiculous ice sculptures. It was all so unnecessary to Aaron.

"Let her celebrate her eldest child's birthday," said Tariq with a smile.

An olive-skinned woman with thick, long black hair approached Aaron and Tariq. She wore a pink silk boatneck dress. She stood right in front of Aaron and rolled her eyes.

"Do you know how many women approached me during this party?" she said. "It's tiring having to speak to them all about you. It's clear that they want to get to you through me."

"Better you than I," said Aaron. She curled her lip to him.

"But are you seeing anyone?"

"If he was, he wouldn't tell you that," said Tariq.

"I absolutely agree," she replied to Tariq and then turned her attention to Aaron. "I don't understand how you and I are siblings. You are so cold, and yet I am so warm."

Aaron barely reacted to her words.

"Maria, it's good to see you again," Tariq said to her with a smile. He leaned closer to her and kissed on her both cheeks.

"Likewise," she replied. Maria was Aaron and Joseph's younger sister. She was studying economics in London. She had come home for Aaron's birthday.

"How are your studies?" Aaron asked her. Maria curled her upper lip before bursting into laughter.

"Oh my dear brother, you are such a bore. It's your birthday party, it's hardly the time to be talking about my studies," she said. "How do you get into relationships?" she teased.

"I don't."

"So you just indulge in fruitless dalliances?"

"Precisely." Aaron did not like to get into serious relationships with women. He found it time consuming and pointless. They always developed feelings for him and wanted to be with him all the time. It was bothersome.

"I can't wait to see the woman you wed," said Maria

"You and I both," Tariq added. Tariq and Maria both laughed. Aaron just shook his head. The queen suddenly approached them. She was with a younger woman.

"Aaron, I have someone I wish to introduce you to," said the queen. She looked at the woman she was with. "This is Salma," she said.

"Greetings, sheikh," she said with a deep curtsey. "It is a pleasure to meet you, and I'd like to wish you a happy birthday." She spoke so elegantly. She was tall and beautiful. He could see why his mother wanted to introduce her to him.

"Thank you," he replied.

"She is the daughter of Prince Hamid of Al Hasidia." The queen started talking about Salma. She spoke highly of her but Aaron found it difficult to pay attention. He was not interested.

As the rest of the evening unfolded, more guests came to speak with Aaron. Sheikhs and ministers came to introduce their daughters to him. There was music, food and media coverage. Aaron was pleased when it came to an end. He was glad to be back in his quarters and away from all the ruckus and invasive guests.

***

"Come in," Aaron called out moments after there was a knock on his office door. The door swung open and in walked Deja wearing a burgundy dress and black high heels. She always knew how to dress elegantly and attractively.

"Good morning, sheikh," she greeted him. "Do you have a moment?" she asked.

"It depends, what brings you to my office?"

"I have the feedback on the southern well."

"Have a seat."

Deja walked over to his desk and sat opposite Aaron. She had her curly hair tied up into a bun. Her fair skin was smooth and had a perfect glow. Aaron noticed that she never wore makeup.

"Based on the calculations, the southern well should have produced a lot of oil," she said.

"I am aware of that," Aaron replied.

"The oil produced didn't match the expected amount. Was the machinery faulty or something?"

"I doubt it."

"Just by looking at this information, it's hard to tell what went wrong. I can only suggest that we use a different drilling method this time," she said to him. Deja was quite right. You couldn't look at the information and simply come up with a reason as to why they weren't able to get enough oil. Knowing that, he had still given her the information so that he could hear what she had to say.

"After we meet with the geologist and drilling manager and we have the well logging results, you can use the data to see which will be the best drilling method," said Aaron.

"Yes, sheikh." Deja nodded.

"My secretary will let you know when the meeting has been set up."

"Okay." Deja nodded. "Did you have a good weekend? How was the event you went to?"

Aaron grunted. "It was fine."

"Just fine? It was your 30th."

Aaron raised an eyebrow. "How did you know?" he asked her.

"It was on the television."

"Oh yeah."

"Happy birthday."

Aaron grunted again in response. He had heard enough of that already.

"Why you weren't excited for your birthday? It's a huge milestone," said Deja.

"It's just like any other day of the year," Aaron replied. Deja raised her eyebrows and shook her head.

"No, it isn't. We should always be grateful and celebrate our birthdays."

Aaron shrugged his shoulders. "These massive celebrations are really a waste of money," he said.

"I don't know, I've never spent too much on my birthdays either," she said. "I always do something low-key with close friends and family."

"I see," he replied.

"I better return to the office, I'm sure Mr. Tadros has something for me to do," said Deja as she rose to her feet. Aaron leaned back in his chair and looked up at Deja. It was a surprise that she was the one ending their conversation. It was usually him that had to cut her off and dismiss her.

Deja looked at him as she pushed the folder towards him. "I guess I should return this to you also," she said. Aaron looked back at her. Her big hazel eyes pulled him in. He found himself not looking away.

The door swung open. "Hello!" Joseph said as he walked in. Deja quickly stood up straight and looked away.

"Joseph," said Aaron.

"Am I interrupting?" Joseph asked as he approached the desk. He looked at Deja from head to toe.

"No, I was just leaving," Deja replied with a smile. She turned on her heel and walked out of the office.

"Who is she?" Joseph asked Aaron.

"Miss Gibson, a new engineer," Aaron replied. "You are late?"

"It's only 10 a.m." Joseph slipped a hand in his pocket. "She's pretty."

Aaron stood up. "You need to come in before nine. Let's go, I'll show you around," he said to him. He intentionally ignored the comment about Deja. He didn't exactly want to talk about her.

"Let's go," Joseph replied.

The two of them walked out of the office. Aaron showed his brother all the different departments. He wanted his brother to see the business that their father and grandfather had worked hard for. He hoped that his brother would take some interest in the business.

They stopped by the elevator. "Thanks for the tour," Joseph said to Aaron. "I have to go."

Aaron raised his eyebrows "Go where?" he asked.

"I have people to meet."

Aaron sighed. "Just don't get yourself into any kind of trouble," he warned. Joseph was always up to no good. He didn't want him to do something that may anger their father.

"Of course I won't," Joseph replied. He walked into the elevator and pressed the button for the ground floor. Aaron slipped his hands in his pockets and turned his head. He saw Deja getting up from her desk. She looked up and found Aaron looking at her. She held his gaze as she walked over to the photocopier. When she reached the photocopier, she shyly looked away. Aaron cleared his throat and headed to his office.

Chapter 14

Deja felt her stomach knot up in response to Aaron's intense gaze. She fiddled around with the photocopier until he was gone. She looked up and sighed with relief. It was the second time they had stared at each other that day. The first time was when she was in his office, and then they were interrupted by Joseph. Deja wondered who Joseph was. He slightly resembled Aaron.

Deja quickly finished photocopying her documents and then filed them. She went to sit down at her desk and carried on with her work. For the rest of the day, she found it difficult to concentrate. Her mind kept drifting back to Aaron. She couldn't get his gaze out of her head. She couldn't stop thinking about how he had stared at her. Thinking about it made her stomach knot up.

Aaron was a handsome and cold crown prince. No good could come out of thinking about him. Deja shook her head and decided to get on with her work.

***

Deja had a burst of mixed emotions when the sheikh's secretary summoned her for a meeting with the sheikh a few days later. She was excited because she assumed that meeting was about their project. It meant that she was getting more work. However, she felt odd and nervous about seeing the sheikh. The last time she had seen him, he was standing by the elevator and looking at her.

She followed the petite brown-haired secretary to the sheikh's office. She knocked on the door and waited for the sheikh's confirmation to enter. After she heard it, she opened the door for Deja.

"Good afternoon, sheikh," Deja greeted him as she walked into the office. He was sitting on the sofas a few feet away from his desk. He wasn't alone, he was with the geologist and the drilling manager; Anwar and Jacob.

"Miss Gibson, please join us," said Aaron. Deja nodded as she made her way over to him. It had been a few days since she had seen or spoken to him. She wondered if he had been on a business trip. Deja sat down at Aaron's right side, opposite Anwar and Jacob.

"Hello gentlemen," she greeted them.

"It's good to see you again, Deja," said Jacob.

"Likewise," Deja replied.

"Jacob brought well and mud log results for the southern well," Aaron said to Deja. "I will need you to interpret them and provide a drilling method."

"Yes, sheikh." Deja nodded as she took the results. She felt excited about finally beginning the project. She was finally going to do calculations and use them to determine the best drilling method.

Anwar started talking about the budget for the project. He rattled off a bunch of figures to the sheikh. As the group continued their discussion, Deja watched Aaron. He oozed confidence and sex appeal. He was just so attractive, so eloquent and so intelligent.

After the meeting, Jacob and Anwar got up and bowed to the sheikh. They walked out of the office leaving Aaron and Deja alone. She turned and faced the sheikh.

"I guess I should return to my office," she said. She didn't know what else to say to him. Aaron raised his eyebrows.

"You're a woman of very few words today," he said to her.

"Is that a good thing or a bad thing?" She couldn't tell because normally he complained about her talking too much but this time he looked amused.

"It makes no difference to me." Aaron pulled his phone out of his pocket and swiped the screen. Deja watched him for a moment. He crossed his dark eyebrows slightly as he looked at the screen. Deja wondered what he was looking at. She wondered if he had a social media account just like normal people. She was curious about what he was like outside the office.

"Why are you staring at me?" Aaron asked Deja. Her eyes widened for a split second. *Damn!* her subconscious swore. The last thing she wanted was to get caught staring at him. He was looking at his phone, so she thought he wouldn't catch her looking.

"I was not staring at you." Deja casually rose to her feet and straightened her skirt. She didn't want him to see her sweat over getting caught.

"Hmm." Aaron grunted as he looked up. Deja turned on her heel and walked out of his office. She placed her hand on her stomach as she headed to her office. She felt it knot up. Being around Aaron gave her butterflies, and she didn't like it. She wanted to suppress that feeling as much as she could.

"Are you really working with the sheikh?" Basil asked Deja as she walked into the office.

"Yes," Deja replied.

"That doesn't make any sense. You haven't been working here long enough for him to notice your talent," Fadi added. Deja walked over to her desk and sat down.

"Did you sleep with him?" Basil asked.

"Watch your mouth!" Kara warned him. Deja frowned and shook her head. That was the very thing she was worried about. She didn't want people to think she had gotten the chance to work with the sheikh through dishonest ways.

"No, I did not sleep with him," Deja replied.

"Well then why is he working with you?" Fadi asked.

"Deja was an outstanding student at MIT. She graduated at the top of our class. Who wouldn't want to work with someone as intelligent as she is?" said Kara.

"There are a lot of intelligent people at this company that haven't gotten the opportunity to work with the sheikh yet," said Basil. Deja shrugged her shoulders.

"You can go and ask him yourself," she said. Mr. Tadros walked into the office and all chatter stopped immediately. Deja was glad that he had walked in. She was fed up with hearing what Basil and Fadi had to say about her working with the sheikh.

"What's the commotion about?" Mr. Tadros asked.

"Nothing," Kara replied.

"Then get on with your work."

Deja sank in her seat. She was glad that Mr. Tadros hadn't walked in earlier because even he wasn't happy about her working with the sheikh. He had been treating her differently since he found out that she was working with the sheikh.

.

Chapter 15

Aaron arrived at work around 11 a.m. the next morning. He walked into his office and found Joseph sitting at his desk with his feet up.

"What are you doing?" Aaron asked him. Joseph looked at the gold Rolex sitting on his wrist.

"Look what time you're strolling into the office," Joseph replied. Aaron shut the door behind him and walked over to the desk.

"I had a meeting." He stood next to Joseph. "Move," he demanded.

"Sure." Joseph got out of Aaron's seat and went to sit at the sofas. Aaron sat down in his chair.

"Why are you here?" Aaron asked his brother.

"You wanted me to come to the office more often."

Aaron turned his head and looked at his brother with one eyebrow raised. "You've come to work?" he asked. He didn't believe that his brother would come on his own accord. Joseph disliked the idea of working at the office every day. He just wanted to travel and party. Aaron laid out some documents of printed sketches of a well and calculations.

"Yes I have. Why is that hard to believe?" Joseph asked.

"Because it's you."

Joseph leaned back in the sofa and put his feet up on the table. "I heard father saying that he wanted to cut me off," he said. Aaron shook his head.

"I warned you," he replied. Joseph flared his nostrils and narrowed his gaze at his older brother. Suddenly there was a soft knock on the door. "Come in," Aaron called out.

"You aren't even asking who it is?" Joseph asked Aaron. Deja walked into the room. "I see, you were expecting her," he added. Aaron didn't bother responding to his brother.

"What brings you to my office?" Aaron asked Deja.

"I have interpreted the well logging results and drafted a drilling method," she said to him. She placed the documents on his desk. Aaron slightly widened his eyes. He was not expecting her to work that fast.

"I will have a look." He took the documents.

"What was your name again?" Joseph asked Deja.

"Deja," she replied. Joseph grunted and nodded.

"You may leave." Aaron dismissed Deja. He didn't want his brother teasing her. He knew that his brother was about to because of the way he grunted.

Joseph liked to flirt and tease women. Although Aaron was impressed by her quick thinking, he wasn't the type to shower people with compliments and praise.

"Yes, sheikh." Deja turned on her heel and headed out of his office. Aaron slightly crossed his eyebrows. Deja had just walked out without bowing her head to him. He realized that she never did so. He was going to have to talk to her about it.

"Deja. There is something interesting about her," said Joseph. Aaron raised an eyebrow and looked at Joseph. "Don't you agree?" he added.

"I have a new project for development of an oil well. You will be working on it from now on."

"What? Why?" Joseph removed his feet from the table and sat up straight.

"I'm busy with the southern well project. Besides, this is your chance to impress father. Surely you don't want him to cut you off and leave you with no money or assets?"

"No." Joseph sulked. He rose to his feet and walked over to Aaron's desk. "Do I at least get an office?" he asked.

"Sure. I'll get one sorted out for you," Aaron replied.

***

Later that day, Aaron sat with his family for dinner. His mother wanted to have dinner with the entire family since they were all in town. Usually Maria would be in London studying, Joseph would be somewhere in the world partying and living a lavish life and Aaron was always traveling on business.

"Joseph came to the office today," Aaron said to his father as he cut into his grilled lamb.

"To do what?" the king asked.

"To work. He has taken on a project."

"Is that so?" the queen breathed. She looked at Joseph in disbelief.

"I will believe it when I see it," said the king.

"Well cheers to that," said Maria before she sipped from her crystal glass. Joseph slightly frowned.

"Yes, I have taken on a project," he said. "I will not be leaving the country for a while. I will stay here and work." Aaron could tell that it was hard for his brother to say those words. He disliked working and staying put in one place. Aaron was proud of his brother.

"It's about time," said the king. He on the other hand did not look impressed.

"Next on the agenda is Aaron's marriage," said Maria. Aaron shot a glance at his sister from the corner of his eye. "I ran into Salma when I was out shopping," she added.

"Who's Salma?" Aaron frowned.

"Prince Hamid's daughter. You met her at the party," said the queen.

"Oh." Aaron shrugged his shoulders. "I met a lot of people at the party," he added. There must have been nothing special about her since he didn't remember her.

"We spoke. She was quite lovely, and her interest in you was quite apparent," said Maria as she smiled at Aaron cheekily.

"She is a lovely woman. I was planning to meet with her again," said the queen. As she started talking about what made Salma the perfect match for Aaron, Aaron stopped listening. He strangely started thinking about Deja. She had boldly suggested changes on the well he was looking at. It was new to Aaron. No one just spoke out to him unless asked to do so.

Aaron also realized that her tone wasn't as formal. She spoke to him as if she were speaking to any ordinary man. She didn't realize how privileged she was to be in his company. She— "Aaron!" his mother called out and disturbed him from his thoughts.

"Yes, Mother," he replied.

"Did you not hear me speaking to you?"

"Sorry, I just have a lot on my mind," he replied.

"Work again." Maria rolled her eyes. The king smiled.

"It's not a bad thing if he is so focused on work," he said. Joseph raised an eyebrow. It was clear that he didn't agree.

"Exactly," Aaron agreed, even though he wasn't thinking about work.

"However, focusing too much on work is a bad thing," said Maria. Both Aaron and the king looked at her as though she had said the strangest thing. The queen smiled and nodded.

"She is right. One must work hard but also take time to enjoy the fruits of life," said the queen.

"Mm-hmm," Maria agreed loudly.

"When will you go to New York?" the queen asked Aaron.

"In a week's time," Aaron replied. Maria shook her head.

"I can't believe that every time you go to New York, it's simply for work," said his little sister. She took a sip of her drink. "New York is the best place for fashion," she added.

"I have no interest in fashion." Every year, Aaron attended a gala in New York. The attendees were business people from oil companies all over the world. The gala was not open to just anyone; only the best and most successful CEOs and business people were invited.

"Will you go alone or with a date?" Maria asked.

"Probably alone," Joseph interjected.

"Take Salma with you," said the queen.

"I'd rather not," said Aaron. He had had only one conversation with her. Therefore, he didn't know her and found no reason for her to accompany him to the gala. If he was to take a woman to the gala, it'd be someone that could be useful to him.

Chapter 16

It was a warm Friday morning. It wasn't too hot; the weather was just right. Deja was happy that it was Friday because she and Kara had plans for the weekend. She looked forward to Saturday morning because she didn't have to wake up so early for work. She could just sleep in.

"Morning Deja," Fadi greeted her as he approached her.

"Hi," she replied. Fadi leaned against her desk.

"Are you meeting with the sheikh today?"

Kara looked up from her desk "Why are you asking?" she asked Fadi. Obviously, she could hear what he was saying as her desk was right next to Deja's.

"He's just curious. Can you blame him?" said Basil as he approached. Deja put her pen down and leaned back in her chair.

"The sheikh hasn't requested to see me," she replied.

"I thought you could go and see him whenever you wanted."

"With what authority?"

"I though you and the sheikh were on informal terms. I'm sure you can go and see him when you want."

Deja crossed her eyebrows as she felt her insides burning up. She hated that Basil and Fadi thought that she was sleeping with Aaron just to get ahead. It was the very thing that she had been worried about.

"Would you mind repeating that?" a deep husky voice sounded. They all turned around and saw Aaron walking into the office.

"Sheikh!" Fadi breathed. Kara and Deja immediately rose from their seats. Fadi and Basil bowed their heads to Aaron. Kara and Deja looked at each other. Kara then bowed her head to the sheikh. Deja felt odd about bowing her head to him, given the fact that she was from a country where they didn't have a monarchy. She awkwardly cocked her head to the side in an attempt to bow.

"Miss Gibson and I are on informal terms? Would you mind elaborating that statement to me?" said Aaron. He stood only a few feet away from them. He wore navy-blue trousers and a navy-blue shirt. No matter what he wore, he looked handsome.

"Sheikh, I didn't mean anything by it. Please forgive me," said Basil.

"I don't appreciate a man that speaks words that he can't own up to. Watch what you say, especially if it involves me."

Deja was happy that she wasn't the one receiving the sheikh's wrath. He looked and sounded intimidating. At the same time, she also found him attractive.

"Yes, sheikh," Fadi and Basil said in unison.

"Miss Gibson never did anything despicable to gain my attention." Aaron turned his head to face Deja. "Come to my office for a moment," he added.

"Yes, sheikh," she said. Aaron turned on his heel and walked out of the room. Deja and Kara looked at each other.

"Well." Kara rubbed her hands together and looked at Basil and Fadi. "That'll teach you not to make assumptions."

Deja didn't bother to say anything to Fadi and Basil. Aaron had already said it all. She was surprised that he defended her. She was happy that he had done that because she didn't like hearing Fadi and Basil talking about her. Now they were probably going to stop because they didn't want to be on the wrong side of the sheikh.

Deja rushed out of her office and headed over to Aaron's. She knocked before she walked in. The sheikh was leaning against his desk. He had his phone in his hand.

"Sheikh," Deja said softly. "You wanted to see me?"

"Yes." Aaron looked up from his phone. "I'm going away for a couple of days."

"Okay." Deja nodded. She wondered why he was telling her. The last time she had commented on him going out of town, he said that it wasn't her business.

"I need you to handle things with the southern well."

"Me?" Deja's hazel eyes widened. "What do you mean handle things?"

"Oversee the project," Aaron said. Deja wanted him to elaborate.

"Oversee, how?"

Aaron slipped his phone into his pocket and crossed his arms over his chest. "Go to the rig and make sure that the drilling is going well, monitor the budgets and do whatever else is needed," he said. He sounded so relaxed.

"Why me?" she asked him. It was such a big responsibility. He was basically leaving her in charge of the project.

"The king wanted you on this project. It's your chance to impress him," he replied. Deja raised her eyebrows. It wasn't about the king. The sheikh was testing her. And she wanted to do well. She wanted to impress him.

"I will do my best," she said to him.

"As you should."

Deja cleared her throat. "I appreciate you, I mean I appreciate what you did earlier with the guys," she said. She wanted to thank him for defending her when Fadi and Basil were saying obscene things about her.

Aaron raised his eyebrows. "I didn't do it for you," he said bluntly. Deja shifted awkwardly.

"Oh." She felt a little disappointed.

"The last thing I want is people whispering about me having inappropriate relations with my employees."

"Yeah." She looked down. She was hoping that he had done that for her. She chastised herself for even thinking that way. Of course he was not defending her, why would he? He was obviously defending himself.

"You sound disappointed," he said. She looked up and met his dark gaze.

"I'm not," she lied. She was slightly disappointed but she was not going to admit that to him. "There is no reason for me to be."

"Deja," he said. Hearing her name on his lips made her insides melt. He never called her by her first name. He always referred to her as Miss Gibson. "I have noticed that you don't address me in the manner that you should," he said.

"I don't understand what you mean," Deja replied.

"You don't bow to me, and you don't seem to care that I am a prince, a crown prince in fact."

"What makes you think that I don't care?" Deja started smiling.

"You don't give me the respect that I deserve. You don't quite realize how lucky you are to even be in the presence of the future king."

Deja let out a laugh. He had to be joking, she thought to herself. Otherwise he was being ridiculous. Deja tucked a curly lock of hair behind her ear and looked at Aaron. He wore a stern facial expression. "Oh, you're serious," she said.

"Of course I am," he said. Deja cleared her throat.

"I do respect you. As for the bowing, it's all new to me."

Aaron raised a dark eyebrow. "You're in an Arabic country. Therefore, you should learn our customs and traditions," he said. Deja shrugged her shoulders.

"I am learning and I do respect your culture. In fact, Kara and I will be going to the royal museum this weekend." She smiled. The royal museum had all the information there was to know about Aaron's family and ancestors. The museum also held precious family possessions handed down each generation.

"Is that supposed to impress me?" Aaron asked with a sad face. Deja shook her head.

"No."

"Well, the royal museum is a great place to start."

"It is, isn't it? I can't wait to see. We–" Deja was barely able to finish speaking. Aaron cut her off as he normally did.

"You may leave. You're starting to talk too much again," he said to her. Deja's left nostril twitched. She felt infuriated every time he cut her off.

"Yes, sheikh," she spat out. She turned on her heel and touched the door handle. Just as she was about to open the door, she heard Aaron's deep husky voice.

"Don't let those two foolish men's words affect your work. You know that my father chose you to work with me because he recognized your talent," he said. Deja turned around and looked at him. "If they or anyone else bothers you about working with me, let me know," he added.

"Okay." Deja nodded. Her stomach knotted up as she walked out of his office. She wasn't sure what to make of what Aaron had just said to her. Earlier he had said that he didn't want people speaking badly of him. However, it was now sounding as though he was looking out for her. Was he starting to warm up to her?

Chapter 17

Deja wore a black dress to her meeting with Jacob and Anwar and other people involved in the southern well project. She felt a little nervous about meeting with them. Aaron had left her in charge of the project. It was a big deal. Deja straightened her dress before she walked into the conference room.

"Good morning, gentlemen," she said as she walked into the room. There were six men in the room. She only recognized Anwar and Jacob.

"Good morning," Jacob greeted her. Deja pulled out the chair from the head of the table and sat down. Jacob and Anwar looked at each other.

"My name is Deja and the sheikh sent me here as he is away on business. I will report the summary of this meeting to him when he returns," she said. Everyone just looked at each other and then back at Deja. "Shall we begin?" she asked.

Deja pulled a notepad and a pen out of her bag. "Can we start with brief introductions?" she asked. They all looked at her as though she was strange.

"I think it would be better if the sheikh was here," said one angry-looking man.

"I'm sorry, I didn't get your name?" Deja replied.

"Mr. Khan," he said proudly. Deja nodded.

"Mr. Khan, the sheikh asked me to conduct this meeting and get the updates. Would you rather I told him that you don't agree with his decision?" she asked. It was clear that they were not pleased that she was there instead of the sheikh. They didn't need to make it so obvious. It was just rude.

Mr. Khan grunted and shifted awkwardly. "How can we even know that the sheikh sent you here? We've never met you before," he said.

"I can vouch for her," said Jacob. "Anwar and I have met Miss Gibson with the sheikh. She is the engineer that came up with the drilling method for this project."

"Fine. Let's just get on with it," said Mr. Khan. He then mumbled something else in Arabic and some of the men laughed. Deja was annoyed by that because she didn't understand what he was saying and it was just rude.

"How is everything going so far?" Deja asked Anwar. She was grateful when he replied properly. He gave detailed information on their progress. Deja wrote down the key points. She didn't want to miss anything when she reported it back to the sheikh. Anwar gave Deja a report on how much money had been spent on the project so far.

Whenever she said anything, only Jacob and Anwar listened to her. The others didn't make eye contact with her nor did they say anything. Deja suggested using different equipment to improve efficiency. They didn't even take her suggestion seriously. They frowned at her every word and groaned in complaint.

"Thank you, gentlemen, for coming," Deja said after the meeting. She was grateful that the meeting had ended. It had been so uncomfortable and awkward. After they had all left, Deja buried her face in her hands.

"Are you okay?" she heard someone's voice. Deja looked up and saw a handsome man standing in the doorway. She had seen him before in Aaron's office.

"I'm fine." Deja smiled. He walked in and sat down at the table with her. "How may I help?" she asked. He extended his hand to her.

"I'm Joseph," he said.

"Hello Joseph." Deja was confused. She was wondering why he was there and why he was introducing himself to her.

"I'm Aaron's younger brother."

Deja's eyes flew wide open. "You are?" she asked. He vaguely resembled Aaron but the thought of him being Aaron's brother hadn't crossed her mind. Joseph nodded.

"I know it's shocking since I'm the better-looking brother." He grinned at her. Deja laughed.

"And the friendlier one," she added.

"Yes, Aaron is quite stiff. He has no sense of humor."

Deja smiled. "Well, it's nice to meet you, Joseph," she said to him. He sighed and leaned back in his chair.

"A new project arose, and Aaron gave it to me to work on, since he's busy with the southern well," he said.

"Oh, you're working on it?"

Joseph nodded. "I have some well-logging results that aren't making sense to me. I was thinking of looking for someone to interpret them for me." Joseph placed some documents on the desk.

"Ah, I can do that for you." Deja took the results.

"That's kind of you." Joseph smiled at her.

"It's kind of my job to interpret well-logging results." She returned his smile.

"How long have you worked here?"

"A month," she said.

"How has it been working with my brother?"

"It's been fine," she said. Working with Aaron wasn't just fine. Deja had found herself feeling all kinds of emotions. He was so cold towards her and he always cut her off. It annoyed her but she found herself excited to see him, and she felt nervous around him.

"Just fine?" Joseph didn't seem to believe her.

"It's a privilege to work with him. A lot of people never get the opportunity to work with him."

Joseph laughed a little. "He's such a perfectionist. He's really hard to please and he never warms up to people," he said. Deja raised her eyebrows.

"He never warms up to people?" She found that odd. Joseph shrugged his shoulders.

"I don't know why he's that way." Joseph rose to his feet. "I look forward to hearing from you with the interpreted results," he said. Deja sprang up to her feet.

"Okay," she said to him. He touched her shoulder.

"I guess I owe you. If you need something, just let me know. My office is a few doors down from Aaron's." Joseph smiled and then headed out of the conference room.

Joseph was different to Aaron. He was friendlier than Aaron. Even Tariq was friendlier than Aaron. It was odd to Deja how the people around Aaron were so different from him. She gathered her stuff and walked out of the conference room. She headed to her office that she shared with Mr. Tadros and all the other people in her little team.

When Deja walked into the office, Fadi and Basil looked at her but didn't say anything. Since the sheikh had warned them, they hadn't said anything about her and the sheikh. Deja walked over to her desk and plonked herself in the chair.

***

Aaron returned on Thursday night from his short business trip. He headed to the office first thing next morning. He needed to check on all the current projects since he had been away. He wondered how Deja had handled the project. He had left her in charge of the southern well because he wanted to see how she would handle it. He wanted to know if she could manage a project on her own or not.

He asked his secretary to call Deja into his office as soon as he arrived. He took off his cream-colored suit jacket and sat down at his desk and waited for Deja. She arrived moments later. She wore high-waisted, loose-fitting khaki trousers and a sky-blue blouse. No matter what she wore, she always looked good. Her curly hair was pulled into a loose bun. She wore tiny stud earrings. She was a beautiful woman, she didn't need to try much to look good.

"Good morning, sheikh," she greeted him. As usual she didn't bow her head to him. "How was your trip?" she asked.

"It was fine. Have a seat," he replied.

"Okay." Deja pulled out the chair from his desk and sat down opposite to him.

"What has been happening with the project?"

Deja sighed before she replied. "It was fine but it could have gone better," she said to him.

"Why?" Aaron asked.

"I just felt a little slighted." She shrugged her shoulders and reported everything that had taken place at the meeting. Aaron was a little bit annoyed at the fact that he had left her in charge but Mr. Khan and the others were not taking her seriously. He was going to have to speak to them about it.

"I see," he replied. "Joseph told me that you helped him with his project," he changed the subject. His younger brother had told him how Deja had helped him with some well-logging results. When she had given him the results, she had also recommended a drilling method which Joseph had decided to use. Aaron actually agreed with her recommendation.

"He did? Oh, I didn't do much," she said.

"That's what you think." He leaned back in his chair and just stared at Deja for a moment. "I need you to accompany me somewhere," he said.

"Where?" Deja's hazel eyes lit up with curiosity. It was amusing to see. He liked seeing her curious or excited.

"To a gala in New York."

"New York City? Oh wow. When is it happening?" It was typical of her to say so much. She couldn't simply say yes or okay.

"We leave tonight. The gala is tomorrow night," Aaron replied. Deja's eyes widened.

"Oh wow. What's the gala for?"

"It's a charity event. The guests are CEOs, board members and sheikhs from different oil companies."

Deja gasped. "Oh, and you want me to be your date? I'm just an engineer," she said.

"I never said date," he replied.

"If I'm accompanying you to such an event, then I am coming as your date. Am I not?"

"So you'll come?" He deliberately ignored her question.

"Sure. I just need to find something to wear; a cocktail dress, I assume."

"Don't worry about that. I'll have someone bring clothes over to the house we'll be staying at."

"Um, I can buy something after work, it's fine."

"I insist."

Deja smiled. "Thank you but I'll be alright. I can find something by tonight. It's no problem. Besides it might be a bit awkward to have you buy me a dress," she said.

"As you wish," he replied. It was refreshing to see a woman that wasn't quick to want to spend his money. All the women that he had been involved with in the past wanted to spend his money.

"What time do we leave and where shall I meet you?" she asked.

"I'll send a car to pick you up in the evening," said Aaron. Deja nodded as she rose to her feet.

"I'll see you later then." She turned on her heel and left the office. Aaron shook his head as she walked out. She still hadn't bowed her head to him.

Chapter 18

"I can't believe you're going to New York with the sheikh," Kara said to Deja.

"You and I both," Deja replied as she zipped up her suitcase. She had packed a dress for the gala and an outfit to wear on her way back from New York. She also packed some toiletries and nightwear.

"Is the sheikh warming up to you?"

"I don't know." Deja crossed her arms over her chest. "He did say that this was for business and I'm not his date," she added. Suddenly the doorbell sounded.

"That must be your driver." Kara rolled her neck.

"Must be." Deja rushed to the front door to check who it was and indeed it was the driver. She grabbed her luggage and headed out the front door. Deja and the driver got into the elevator together and headed downstairs to the apartment lobby.

They walked out of the building and headed over to the car. The driver opened the trunk and put Deja's suitcase in. He then opened the car door for her. "Thank you," she said to him as she got into the back seat of the car. He got into the front seat and then drove off.

They arrived at the private airstrip about fifteen minutes later. Deja got out of the car and stared at the huge private jet on the airstrip. Whenever she took a plane somewhere, it was always in the economy section. She had never flown first class and now here she was getting ready to fly on a private jet. She looked at herself; she was wearing leggings and a hoodie. She started to regret her outfit. She thought maybe she should have dressed up a little. Kara had told her to but she had refused. She always liked to wear comfortable clothes when she flew but this time was different. She was flying with the sheikh.

"Good evening, Miss Gibson," a neatly dressed flight attendant greeted her.

"Hello," Deja replied.

"The sheikh is waiting for you inside."

"Okay." Deja walked up the stairs and into the jet. The jet was quite spacious. The interior was brown and beige. Deja walked down the wide aisle and headed over to Aaron. The sheikh was sitting in a large, comfortable-looking beige chair. He was wearing a navy-blue long-sleeved top and blue tracksuit. Aaron looked up.

"Hi," Deja greeted him.

"Hello," he replied. "Have a seat." He gestured towards the seat opposite him.

Deja and Aaron buckled their seatbelts. The flight attendant rattled off some safety instructions, and then they were off moments later. Deja drank in her surroundings. She had never been in such a luxury plane before. A month ago, if someone told her that she would be flying in a private jet with the crown prince of Al Nurat, she would have never believed them.

"It'll be a long flight," said Aaron. "If you want to sleep or use the restroom, just go through this brown door." Deja nodded.

"It's weird being on a private jet," she said.

"How?" Aaron was looking at his tablet.

"I don't know. It just is." Deja sank into her chair. It was so comfortable. "You seem different to your brother."

"And I am grateful for that," he spoke without looking up from his tablet. Deja was looking at him. She noticed that he had thick eyelashes. When she was younger, she wanted thicker and longer lashes. Everything about Aaron was just perfect. He was just so handsome, tall, muscular, he had a beautiful voice and amazing skin.

"Why?" Deja was amused.

"We are just very different."

"It must be nice to have a brother though," she said. "I only have two sisters."

"You have siblings?" Aaron looked up from his tablet.

"Yeah." Deja nodded. "One older and one younger. It's not easy being the one in the middle."

"The middle child is the problem child," Aaron said softly. Deja let out a laugh. Aaron was actually joking with her. It was shocking but refreshing.

"I'm not a problem child. They just seem to argue a lot and then I get dragged into the mess."

"I find it hard to believe that you have no part in the *mess*."

Deja's eyes widened. "Why?" she asked him. Aaron raised an eyebrow and leaned back in his chair.

"You seem a little mischievous," he said.

"Mischievous?"

Aaron nodded. "The first time I met you, you jumped up like you were going to fight me." Aaron laughed softly. "I wondered why you were so brave," he added.

"Is that what I looked like?" Deja laughed. "Oh, that was a scary experience. All I wanted to do was tour the desert but then I ended up being kidnapped." Deja sighed. Aaron shook his head.

"For months, there had been reports of people getting abducted around that area. I was glad that I finally caught those nomads."

"As the crown prince, what were you doing there? Wouldn't you just send your men?"

"I was frustrated. The police hadn't been able to catch them. So, I took matters into my own hands."

Deja was impressed that Aaron was the type of man that would go and do something if he felt that it was not getting done right. Since he was a prince, she'd have expected him to send people instead.

The flight attendant brought them refreshments. Aaron and Deja ate as they talked about different things. For the first time ever, Deja was asking Aaron questions and he was replying. Aaron actually indulged in a conversation with Deja. It was nice to speak to him and get to see a different side of him.

They arrived in New York around 2 a.m. Deja was tired from the 12-hour journey. There was a car waiting for them when they got off the plane. The car drove them to Aaron's penthouse. "This is your place?" she asked Aaron as they entered a large room with wooden floors.

"Yes," Aaron replied.

"Why would you have a penthouse that you don't even use?"

"I use it when I come to New York. Hotels can get hectic."

Deja was speechless. It seemed like a waste of money to her but then again, he was wealthy enough to own properties around the world. She gaped at her surroundings. The penthouse had high ceilings and large windows. It was furnished with expensive furniture. The driver brought in Deja's luggage from the car. He bowed his head to Aaron before he left.

"I'll show you to the guest bedroom," said Aaron.

"I am quite tired actually," Deja replied. She was about to reach for her suitcase when Aaron grabbed the handle. He dragged it and headed down the hall. Deja smiled to herself as she followed behind him.

"This is it," he said as he came to a halt outside a door. "Go in and get some rest."

Deja nodded. "Good night," she said to him. Aaron just walked off without responding. Deja opened the door and walked into the room. The light switch was just by the door. She switched it on and stared at the room. It resembled a hotel room. She walked over to the massive king-sized bed and threw herself on it. She lay on her back and stared at the chandelier hanging above her.

She still couldn't believe that she was staying at an expensive penthouse in New York with the sheikh. It was surreal. Deja sighed and closed her eyes. She was very tired from the long journey. She hadn't slept much on the jet because she didn't want to snore or do something embarrassing in front of Aaron. So, she forced herself to stay awake and kept herself busy on her phone and talking to Aaron.

Chapter 19

Aaron was sitting at the breakfast table reading a newspaper when Deja stumbled into the kitchen. He watched her stretching and yawning. She was wearing blue pajama shorts and a blue T-shirt.

"Good morning," she greeted him as she joined him at the table.

"Morning," he replied. He eyed her messy hair. "I guess you were really tired," he added. She yawned and smiled.

"I was," she replied.

"Eat." He returned his attention to the newspaper. Deja poured coffee into an empty porcelain mug and then added sugar. She inhaled the scent before she took a sip.

"Did you cook?" she asked.

"No." Aaron crossed his eyebrows. He had never cooked anything in his life, unless microwaving counted as cooking. "I have a maid," he added.

"Oh." Deja laughed a little. "That makes more sense. What time does the gala start?" she asked him.

"7 p.m."

"What do we do until then?"

"Do whatever you want. I have matters to attend to."

"Okay." Deja nodded. Aaron was used to eating breakfast alone. And if not alone, then with his family. Strangely it felt normal to dine with Deja. She was oddly interesting. They had spent most of their journey to New York talking.

"I'm leaving," Aaron said to Deja when he was finished eating.

"Okay, see you later." Deja smiled at him. Aaron gave her half a smile and left the kitchen.

***

Aaron waited for Deja in the living room. It was almost time for them to leave for the gala and she still hadn't finished getting ready. He wondered what was taking so long. He hoped that she was going to wear something decent, since she had refused his offer to get her something. He was going to obviously hire the best designers in New York to come and dress her.

"Deja!" he called out. It was so unlike him to yell but she was taking forever. "Hurry up!" he added.

"I'm almost done," she called back.

Deja walked out moments later. She was wearing a navy-blue satin dress. It hugged her torso and then flared out from her waist to her ankles. Her curly hair was pinned up. She wore pearl stud earrings. Aaron just stood there staring at her. Deja looked gorgeous.

"I'm done now," she said to him. Aaron eyed her from head to toe. Her fair skin had a beautiful glow. It looked so amazing and alluring. "Sheikh?" Deja said. Aaron had just been staring at her and not saying anything.

"Let's go." He cleared his throat and headed towards the front door. Deja followed him out. Their driver was waiting for them outside the car. He opened the door for them. Aaron let Deja get into the car first and then he got in and sat next to her.

"We're finally leaving," said Aaron. "It took you so long to get ready."

"It takes a long time to fix my hair," she replied. Aaron looked at her hair and raised his eyebrows.

"Really?" he didn't believe her.

"Yeah. I have long curly hair. It's hard to maintain."

Aaron laughed. "I don't believe that hair is that hard to maintain," he said. Deja gasped and looked at him.

"That is because you're a man, and you have straight hair," she replied.

"How long does it take you to style?" He was intrigued.

"I deep condition for at least half an hour, then it takes fifteen to twenty minutes to blow dry. Styling takes at least fifteen minutes more," she explained.

"So, more than an hour?" he asked.

"Yes. And since it's so thick, I need to moisturize daily."

Aaron shook his head. "Sounds like a nightmare," he said.

"It is." Deja laced her fingers together. Aaron noticed that she also had done her nails. She had blue nail polish on.

"It's nice to be a man," said Aaron. They both laughed. They arrived at the venue half an hour later. They'd have arrived much sooner if it weren't for the New York traffic. Their car pulled up right at the front of the venue.

Deja sighed loudly. "I've never been to a gala," she said. Aaron looked at her and raised an eyebrow.

"Are you nervous?" he asked her.

"No."

"You look nervous."

"Okay maybe a little but I'm excited too," she admitted.

"It'll be fine. I just view it as business," Aaron replied. "Just try not to talk too much."

Deja gasped. "I don't talk too much," she said.

"Yes you do."

She frowned at him a little. "You're so mean," she mumbled as she turned away. She started rummaging through her purse. Aaron smiled. She was adorable.

"What are you doing? We need to get out," he said to her.

"Okay, one second." She pulled out a tiny glass bottle and sprayed her wrists, behind her ears and under her armpits. She put it back in her purse and then fished out some breath mints. She put one in her mouth and then turned to look at Aaron. "Would you like one?" she asked him. Aaron was just staring at her in amusement.

"No," he replied. She put them back in her purse.

"Okay, I'm ready. Let's do it."

Aaron shook his head and opened the door. Deja was just from another planet. She was different to every woman he had ever been around. She talked too much, she was eccentric, she had no respect for him or his culture but she was beautiful, smart and amusing. He was glad that he had chosen her to attend the gala with him.

Chapter 20

Deja and Aaron walked into the ballroom filled with well-dressed people. The women wore beautiful expensive dresses and jewelry. The men were dressed in fine suits or tuxedos. However, none of the men bested Aaron. He wore a crisp white shirt, black trousers, black bow tie and a navy-blue velvet blazer with silk lining. He completed the outfit with expensive designer velvet loafers. His hair was parted on the left side and neatly brushed back. His beard was neatly shaped and brushed.

Aaron looked breathtaking and Deja couldn't believe that she was going to spend the weekend with him. They had spent twelve hours together on the private jet and then spent a night together... in separate rooms. If her co-workers heard about that, they'd definitely gossip non-stop.

As Deja and Aaron walked into the room, heads turned and eyes stared. Some women gushed over Aaron. Deja wanted to link her arm with Aaron's arm but she couldn't do that. She was there for business with Aaron and not as a *couple* on a *date*.

A group of men immediately approached Aaron and Deja. They bowed their heads to sheikh and greeted him. They looked so happy to see him. As usual,

Aaron wasn't all that friendly. He greeted them and talked to them but he wasn't as smiley as they were. He maintained a stern facial expression. He introduced Deja to them as an engineer at his company that he was working with on a project. That was true but Deja was a little bit disappointed. He could have introduced her as a friend or something.

A little while later, everyone sat down at different tables for dinner. Deja's eyes almost popped out of her head when Aaron pulled out the chair for her. She didn't want to react too much because they were in front of people. So, instead, she just smiled at him and thanked him. She sat down in the chair, and Aaron tucked her in. Then he sat down next to her.

"Hello," an olive-skinned lady greeted Deja as she sat down next to her. She had sandy blond hair that was styled into a neat up-do. She had a small black mole by her nose.

"Hi." Deja smiled at her.

"Nina." She extended her hand out for a handshake. Deja shook her hand.

"Deja," she introduced herself.

"You came with the sheikh?" Nina asked her.

"Yes, we're colleagues."

"Just colleagues?" She didn't seem to believe Deja.

"Yes. Just colleagues," Deja replied.

Nina nodded. "That's my husband sitting next to the sheikh, so that he can kiss up to the sheikh," she said and shook her head. Deja laughed a little.

As the evening progressed, Deja and Nina talked more. Deja was happy that she had someone to talk to because Aaron was occupied. A lot of people were taking turns to approach Aaron. They wanted his attention. Deja wanted his attention too but they were there for business. So, she was going to let Aaron interact with other business people and not distract him.

At some point during the evening, Aaron leaned closer to Deja "Are you alright?" he asked. Deja inhaled sharply because of Aaron's sudden closeness to her. She turned to face him and met his dark gaze. His face was a few inches away from hers. Deja's heart started racing fast.

"I'm okay," Deja replied.

"Good." His gaze dropped to her lips and then back up to her eyes. "I'm just going to speak with someone. When I return we'll leave," he added. Deja nodded and then watched him walk away. He had left at the perfect time because if he stayed that close to her for longer, she was going to explode.

She turned her attention away from Aaron and took a sip of her drink. She made eye contact with Nina's husband. "Are you enjoying the evening?" he asked her.

"Yes I am," Deja replied with a smile.

"The sheikh values you."

"What makes you say that?"

"He mentioned how hard-working and intelligent you are." He smiled and took a sip of his drink. "You graduated at the top of your class at MIT?" he asked.

"I did." Deja was so confused. Had Aaron actually spoken highly of her to someone? It was so unbelievable. "Did the sheikh tell you that?" she asked him. Nina's husband nodded. Deja didn't know what to say. Whenever she was with the sheikh, he never complimented her. He was always so cold and abrupt with her.

Aaron returned moments later. Deja bid her farewell to Nina and her husband. Those were the only people that had bothered to speak to her. The rest had had their attention on Aaron only.

One their way out of the ballroom, a photographer approached them and asked for a picture. Deja looked at Aaron and waited for him to respond.

"Sure," Aaron said as he snaked his arm around Deja's waist. She looked at the camera and smiled awkwardly. She tried so hard not to look nervous because she was shocked about Aaron having his arm around her waist.

The photographer snapped a few shots and then thanked them when he was finished. Aaron said nothing. He just walked off. Deja smiled at the photographer and then followed Aaron to the car.

"You were rather quiet tonight," Aaron said to Deja as they headed back to his penthouse.

"I thought that was what you wanted," she said to him. He looked her up and down and then just looked away. She couldn't guess why he had done that or what he was thinking. He was just so hard to predict.

Deja was quick to take her shoes off when they arrived back at the penthouse. Her small toes were starting to hurt because she had been wearing new shoes for a while. She had bought a new dress and shoes especially for the gala. She wanted to look good for Aaron. Since she was his date at the gala, she didn't want to embarrass him by not looking her best.

"That feels good," said Deja as she freed her feet from her five-inch heels. Aaron shook his head.

"I don't even understand why women wear that type of shoes," he said as he shut the front door. They started walking down the hall where the bedrooms were.

"Neither do I." Deja sighed. "We have to wear ridiculous things just to look good."

"As long as you look good. The worst thing is a woman that doesn't know how to look after herself."

Deja laughed. "You're one of those guys," she said.

"What do you mean by *those guys*?"

"That care about looks."

"Everyone cares about looks."

Deja let out a laugh. "Some care about them more than others," she said. They stopped in front of the guest room that Deja was staying in.

"True." Aaron slipped his hands in his pockets and stared down at Deja. The way he looked at her made her speechless and nervous. She didn't know what to say or do. Silence stretched between them.

"Um, good… night?" she said. She could barely get the words out. Aaron leaned closer to her and dipped his head. Before Deja could say or do anything, his lips were pressed against her lips. She inhaled sharply and froze for a second.

He was kissing her.

Deja placed one hand on his chest and kissed him back. His lips were so soft, and he smelled so good. He slowly and gently kissed her.

Aaron held her waist with one hand and pulled her even closer to him as he deepened the kiss. Deja clutched his shirt as her knees buckled. The softness of his lips, the feeling of his tongue in her mouth, the feeling of his rock-hard chest against hers, his manly scent and the feeling of his fingers caressing her lower back was all too much for her. Standing unsupported was becoming impossible.

Aaron broke off the kiss. "Goodnight," he said to her.

"I... th... wh... huh." Deja could barely get any words out. Her brain and body were frozen from the earth-shattering pleasure she had just experienced. Aaron turned on his heel and walked off.

Chapter 21

"Welcome back!" Kara yelled as she kicked Deja's bedroom door open. She rushed into Deja's bedroom and jumped on her bed.

"Kara," Deja complained. She had arrived from New York around 4 p.m. Al Nurat time and then went to bed. She was so tired after the twelve-hour flight and she was jet-lagged.

"How was New York? You have to get up and tell me everything."

As much as Deja wanted to sleep, she needed to talk to Kara. She wanted to tell her everything that had happened in New York.

"Okay." Deja sat up and started talking. Kara stared at her with a wide-eyed expression and giggled as Deja told her everything that happened on her little trip to New York. When it came to talking about the kiss, Deja paused for a second. She still didn't know why Aaron had kissed her. They had shared an incredible kiss and then went to their separate bedrooms. The next day, Aaron hadn't talked about it nor had he tried to kiss her again. They just traveled back to Al Nurat.

"He just leaned in and kissed me. Then he went to bed," said Deja. "That's all that happened." She sighed.

"What?" Kara spat out. "The sheikh kissed you, and you're saying it as if it's not a big deal?"

"It's not." Deja threw herself backwards and landed on her pillows.

"Are we talking about the sheikh that doesn't even hold a personal conversation with you, and refused to hold you when you were falling over?"

"Yes, that one."

"I can't believe this."

"Neither can I." Deja rolled to her side and rested on her elbow. "I just don't know why he kissed me. It was just so random, and now we aren't even talking about it," she added. She wished that she could get inside his mind and see what he was thinking.

"Maybe he's always been attracted to you," said Kara.

"I doubt that."

"I don't think that he's the type of man to do things randomly. He definitely thinks things through before acting."

"Then why is he acting as if nothing has happened? We were on the jet for twelve hours and he didn't talk about it nor did he try to kiss me again. He just spent most of the time on his tablet reading." Thinking about it was frustrating Deja even more.

"You could ask him about it," said Kara.

"I could."

"But?"

"I don't know what to say or how to say it. Kara, it's just so embarrassing. I don't want him to think that I like him."

"And you don't?"

"No." Deja covered herself with the duvet cover.

"Deja!" Kara giggled as she tried to pull the covers away from Deja. "You're in love with the sheikh?"

"I never said that." Deja pulled the covers from her face.

"Then what are you saying?"

"It's just a little crush. It'll pass." Deja sprang out of bed. "I'm hungry," she said as she headed for the door.

"What if it doesn't pass?" Kara followed her out of the room. They both headed to the kitchen.

"It'll have to because this will not end well. He's a crown prince and I'm just a normal woman. I'm sure he has plenty of women vying for his attention."

"Maybe, but that doesn't mean that he wants them."

Deja shrugged her shoulders and bit into a cinnamon bun. It'd be better for her if she just got over the sheikh. Maybe he wasn't talking to her about the kiss because he regretted it. Maybe he wanted to act as though nothing had happened and just move on with his life.

***

Maria knocked on Aaron's bedroom door before she walked in "Hey big brother," she said. Aaron was laying on his bed.

"You're still here," he said. He thought his sister would have returned to London for the rest of the semester.

"Yes, there's only a week left to the semester. There's no point in me returning now." She stood right next to his bed. "How was your trip to New York?" she asked.

"Fine," he replied. He was little bit jet-lagged and he just wanted to rest. "I'll talk to you later," he said to her.

"Who's she?" She swiped her phone and put it right in his face. Aaron looked at the screen. There was a picture of him and Deja at the gala.

"Deja," Aaron replied.

"That's whom you took to the gala with you?"

"Yes."

144

"She's beautiful." Maria looked at him with a mischievous look on her face.

"She's a co-worker," Aaron replied.

"I don't believe that."

"She is."

"Look how you have your arm at her waist." Maria looked at the screen. "You look good together," she added. Aaron remembered when the picture was taken. They were on their way out of the venue. He had wrapped his arm around her waist. When the picture was taken, he let go and walked off, even though he didn't want to. He wanted to hold her.

"Can you leave my room? I need to rest," he said to her.

"Mother was asking for you," said Maria.

"Why?"

"Salma is here."

Aaron sat up. "And what does that have to do with me?" he asked.

"She's probably here to see you. That's why mother is asking you to come downstairs."

Aaron sighed and ran his hand through his hair. He really didn't want to sit down with Salma and have a meaningless conversation. He just wanted to rest. He reluctantly stood up and slipped his house slippers on.

"Are you going downstairs in your slippers?" Maria asked him.

"Yes." He slipped his hands into his linen trousers and headed for the door. Maria followed him out.

"It's unlike you to roam the house in slippers. You really don't care about Salma, do you?"

"No, but it has nothing to do with my slippers. I'm just tired and can't be bothered to get dress for an uninvited guest," he replied. The two of them headed downstairs.

Their mother was sitting in the drawing room with Salma. Salma rose to her feet and bowed her head to the sheikh as he walked into the room. "Good afternoon, sheikh," she greeted him.

"Hello." Aaron sat down at the sofas opposite his mother. Salma sat down after Aaron was seated. She was sitting next to his mother and opposite him.

"Thank you for coming to join us," said the queen. "You must be tired from your long trip."

"I am," Aaron replied. Maria sat down next to him.

"Salma dropped by and I thought it would be nice if you could have tea with us." She reached out for the glass teapot and poured out some black tea for Aaron.

"Oh, he doesn't mind," said Maria.

His mother and Salma started gushing over some charity work that she had done. Aaron was not amused. Anyone could do charity work. It wasn't as if she had done the impossible. The more Salma spoke, the more Aaron found her obnoxious. She had such a gentle tone which was annoying him. She said all the right things and blushed every time Aaron looked at her or spoke to her.

She was the opposite of Deja. Deja spoke her mind and never beat around the bush. She wasn't as gentle as Salma was. She was far more interesting and her lips were soft. Aaron couldn't stop thinking about their kiss. He wanted to kiss her again but he knew that doing so would complicate things. She was a new employee at his company. People were already talking about her sleeping with Aaron to get ahead. What would they say if they knew that he was interested in her?

The last thing Aaron wanted was to make things more difficult for her at the company. She had a bright future ahead of her. Deja was very intelligent and Aaron knew that she was going to be a great asset for the company. He didn't want her reputation to tarred by his feelings or infatuation or whatever it was that he felt towards her.

Going to New York with Deja had showed him a different side of her. He had learned about her family, background, childhood and lots of other things about her. They had spent their journey from Al Nurat to New York talking. He had never spent that much time talking to anyone in one sitting. He wasn't much of a talker. And yet he had spoken to Deja for that long.

"We're hosting an event at the palace in a couple of weeks," the queen said to Salma.

"What kind of event?" she asked.

"Every year, we honor our best employees and give out awards. I'd like for you to attend."

"I'd be honored to."

"The legendary annual Beshara awards. I think it'll be very interesting this year," said Maria with a smirk across her face.

"What makes you say that?" her mother asked.

"We have some rather interesting employees this year."

"Do we?"

"Yes." Maria looked at Aaron and wiggled her eyebrows. He knew that she was referring to Deja because they had spoken about her minutes ago. Aaron just narrowed his gaze at his sister and looked away.

"It sounds like an interesting event. I can't wait," said Salma. She smiled and tucked a lock of hair behind her ear. Aaron broke eye contact and looked away. He wasn't interested in talking to Salma.

She just wasn't Deja.

Chapter 22

Aaron watched Deja walking towards him. "What brings you here?" he asked her. She stopped right in front of his desk.

"Why did you kiss me?" she asked.

"Excuse me?"

It had been two weeks since Aaron and Deja had returned from New York. She hadn't brought up the kiss nor had she tried to kiss him. He thought that she was over it and had forgotten about it. Aaron was surprised that Deja was bringing it up now.

"You randomly kissed me and then never spoke about it," said Deja. Aaron raised his eyebrows.

"You never spoke to me either."

"YOU kissed ME," she emphasized her point. "And then you didn't talk about it. You acted as though nothing had happened."

"Did you come here to talk to me about that?"

"Yes." She looked somewhat nervous. Aaron leaned back in his chair. He was amused. "Can you blame me? For two weeks, you've acted as though nothing happened," she added. Aaron said nothing. He just continued to stare at her.

"Why… why are you looking at me like that?" she asked him. Aaron rose to his feet.

"So, for the past two weeks, you've been thinking about me," he said to her as he walked around the desk.

"Yes, er no. That's not what I said." She was fumbling her words. Aaron stood inches away from her. Her forehead reached his collarbone. She cleared her throat and looked up at him.

"Then what are you saying?" he asked.

"I want to know why you kissed me."

"I wanted to."

"So, now you don't want to kiss me again?" Deja tucked a lock of hair behind her ear and looked down. Aaron caressed her cheek with the back of his hand.

"I want to," he said. He hadn't stopped thinking about her since he kissed her. It had taken a lot for him not to kiss her every time they were alone. "I had to stay away from you for your own good," he said to her.

"What?" Deja looked up and crossed her eyebrows. "That doesn't make sense," she said to him.

"It does. The last thing I wanted was for your colleagues to whisper about you."

Deja rolled her eyes. "They started doing that long before you kissed me," she said.

"You keep saying that I kissed you, as if you didn't kiss me back," he replied as he put his hands on her waist and pulled her closer to him. Deja giggled.

"You initiated and controlled the kiss," she said shyly. She wasn't usually a shy person but she was now, it was adorable.

Aaron grunted in response. He lowered his head and pressed his lips against hers. It felt as though he hadn't kissed her in centuries. He had really missed kissing her. He held her even closer to him as he kissed her.

Deja wrapped her arms around his neck. Aaron broke off the kiss and searched her big hazel eyes. "You must be happy now," he teased. Deja pushed him away playfully.

"Why would I be happy? If anyone should be happy, it's you, Aaron. You're the one that kissed me just now. You must have been thinking about kissing me all this time," she said. Aaron raised his eyebrows.

"Aaron, huh," he said. It was the first time she had called him by his first name. Deja smiled and looked away guiltily. Aaron kissed her jaw. "I have been thinking about kissing you," he admitted.

"Then you should have." Deja looked at him and kissed him.

A knock on the door disturbed them flirting. It was the sheikh's secretary. She was there with a couple of engineers that Aaron was meeting up with.

"I better go," said Deja. She smiled at Aaron and walked over to the door. She opened it and walked out of Aaron's office.

"Come in, gentlemen," Aaron said to the engineers.

***

Deja and Kara entered the Beshara palace. They along with other employees had been invited to the palace for the annual Beshara awards. Deja felt both nervous and excited about going to the palace. While it was intriguing to enter a palace, she was also going to Aaron's home.

Upon entering the large ballroom, Deja was taken aback. The room was beautiful. It had very high ceilings. There was a massive crystal chandelier hanging from the ceiling. The furniture looked very expensive. The floor was made of white marble.

"Deja?" a soft voice called out her name. Deja turned her head towards the voice. A tall, beautiful olive-skinned woman stood before her. She had long, thick black hair. She was wearing a yellow dress.

"Hi." Deja didn't recognize her.

"I'm Maria." She extended her hand for a handshake.

"Hi Maria." Deja shook her hand. Deja was confused. She didn't know who Maria was and how she knew her.

"I'm Aaron's younger sister," she said with a smile. Kara's eyes widened. She looked at Deja with amusement.

"Oh, you don't look like him," said Deja.

"Yeah, people say that I'm the best-looking sibling." Maria laughed. "I'm joking," she said. Deja laughed with her.

"How did you know me?"

"I saw a picture of you and my brother at the gala. Then I asked him who you were."

"Ah." Deja smiled. "And this is Kara."

"How are you?" Maria asked Deja and Kara.

"Good," they both answered.

"It's crazy, getting invited to the palace," said Kara. Maria smiled.

"It's nice to meet you." Maria kissed Deja on both cheeks before she walked off. Kara and Deja looked at each other.

"It's nice to meet you," Kara said to Deja with a smirk on her face.

"He probably told her that we're colleagues. Which is the truth," said Deja.

"Colleagues that kiss." Kara pouted. Deja shook her head.

As the afternoon progressed, they sat down at the fancy tables and had lunch. Then after lunch, the awards were presented. Deja was surprised to be given an award for the best new employee. The king handed the glass plaque to her with a smile of satisfaction on his face. He said that he knew from the start that she was going to be a great asset to the company. She had helped both his sons on their projects. He was proud to have her working at his company.

After the handing out of the awards, Aaron made a little speech about wanting to see the company thrive. Deja could barely concentrate on what he was saying because he looked so handsome. He was dressed in a white collarless shirt with golden embroidery and loose-fitting white trousers.

"Many of you were waiting for me to wed," he announced. Deja and Kara looked at each other. They were both surprised to hear him talking about marriage all of a sudden. "I have found the woman I wish to marry," he added. Deja's eyes widened. What woman? She didn't know that he was even looking. He hadn't mentioned anything about marriage.

"Deja Gibson is the woman I wish to take as my future wife and queen," he said. "She's beautiful and intelligent. I'd be lucky to have her as my wife."

Chapter 23

"Thank you all for attending this event," said the queen. "My family and I have other matters to attend to. Please stay and enjoy the food and music," she added. Aaron looked across the room and saw Deja's shocked face. He wanted to speak to her. She must have been shocked to hear that he wanted to marry her. Shocked and happy. Who wouldn't want to marry him?

"We hope that you continue to work with us and help our company flourish," said the king. He smiled and then exited the room.

"Let's go," the queen whispered in Aaron's ear. Aaron and his mother followed the king out of the room. Maria and Joseph looked at each other with shocked faces before they also left the room.

Aaron and his family headed to his parents' quarters in silence. His mother didn't say anything until they were at the other end of the palace and away from the guests.

"Have you lost your mind?" the queen said to Aaron as soon as they were in the king and queen's heavily guarded quarters.

"Why do you ask me that?" Aaron asked his mother.

"You want to marry Deja? What was that about?"

"Yeah, Aaron, that was very random," said Joseph. He looked just as shocked as the king did. Maria crossed her arms over her chest.

"You better have a good reason for embarrassing us in front of everyone like that," said the king.

"I didn't mean to embarrass anyone. You wanted me to get married, and so I found a woman that I want to get married to," said Aaron. His mother closed her eyes and shook her head.

"You chose a non-Arabic woman?" she said. Aaron shrugged his shoulders. He hadn't thought about her heritage. He just thought that if he had to marry someone, then it'd be Deja. She was the only person that wasn't related to him that spoke their mind to him. She wasn't afraid to disagree with Aaron. She was also very intelligent and would make a great asset to Beshara Oils. She was beautiful and entertaining.

"I didn't think about that," Aaron admitted.

"That is the problem, you didn't think," said the king. "How will you undo what you just did?"

"I didn't do anything wrong. I simply announced my engagement to the public."

The queen ran her hand through her hair. "That's not the way to do it. You could have told us first before you told everyone," she said.

"Why did not you at least pick Salma?" the king asked.

"Exactly. She is a well-mannered woman from a good family," the queen added.

"I am not interested in her," said Aaron.

"I did notice that there was no chemistry between them," Maria interjected. Her parents looked at her as though she had lost her mind.

"Maria, don't get involved," said Joseph.

"I'm just saying, it was very obvious that Aaron wasn't interested in Salma from the start."

"It would have been better if he had said that rather than announcing his engagement in front of her," said the queen as she placed her hand on her heart. "She must have been so shocked and upset," she added.

"Why would she be upset? I never promised to marry her," said Aaron.

"We're not getting anywhere here," said his father. "The bottom line is you aren't getting married to Deja. She's not Arabic nor does she come from a prestigious family."

Maria and Aaron widened their eyes.

"That's cold," Maria mumbled.

"Do I really have to marry an Arabic woman? I don't think that's important," said Aaron.

"Yes, it's important. You're going to be the king. You need to marry a woman that will help strengthen your reign. A woman that knows our culture and traditions," said his mother.

"She can learn."

"Ha! An American?" said his father. "That'll be easy," he said sarcastically.

"You have to give her a chance."

"You have to undo what you did. Tell Deja that you will not marry her, and propose to Salma instead," the king said sternly. He turned on his heel and walked off.

***

Deja was in the kitchen when she heard the doorbell. "I'll get it," Kara called out. Deja took a bite out of her cupcake. She chewed as she headed out of the kitchen. Just as she was about to ask who it was, she found Kara standing in the passage with Aaron.

"Aaron," said Deja. She wiped the cupcake icing from her lips. She wanted to talk to Aaron badly but she didn't want him to see her in a baggy T-shirt, loose-fitting shorts and icing on her lips.

"Deja." He smiled as he closed the distance between them. He kissed her on both cheeks.

"I don't remember telling you where I lived."

"Do you think that I wouldn't be able to find where you live if I wanted?"

Deja rolled her eyes at herself. Of course Aaron could find out her address. "Well, it's good that you're here. We need to talk," she said.

"I'll leave you guys alone." Kara walked off.

"Why did you say that you'd marry me? In front of everyone, without talking to me. I didn't even know that you were looking for a wife."

Aaron smiled. "You have so much to say," he said.

"Of course I do."

"I want to marry you."

"What? How can you even say that? We've never been on a date. You've never even bought me flowers," she spat out. She was so confused. How could he suddenly want to marry her? Aaron grabbed her waist and pulled her closer to him. "What are you doing?" she asked him. Aaron caressed her cheek with the back of his hand.

"Don't you have feelings for me?" he asked.

"I do but it doesn't work like that. Just because I like you doesn't mean that I'll just marry you."

Aaron kissed her cheek. "I want you," he said. He started kissing her neck.

"Aaron." She was finding it difficult to concentrate on what she was saying. "We've never even had a couple's vacation or had coffee together," she said. Aaron pressed a soft kiss against her lips.

"Okay," he said to her. "I'll see you tomorrow." He turned on his heel and headed towards the front door. Deja was left standing in the passage feeling confused.

The next morning, some of her confusion was cleared up when she received a massive bouquet of roses from Aaron. With the roses came a note asking her to join him for dinner later that day. Deja smiled as she sniffed the roses.

"Are they from the sheikh?" Kara asked. Deja nodded. "You have to admit, his proposal to you was kind of romantic," Kara added.

"How?"

"He said it right in front of everyone. Like he didn't even care what anyone thought."

Deja shook her head. "He never spoke to me about marriage. It was just so out of the blue but I have to admit that I am entertaining the idea of marrying him," she said shyly. Kara grinned and clapped her hands.

"The two of you have an interesting bond. You met in the desert after you were kidnapped, and then you ended up working at the same company. FATE!!!"

Was it really fate? Deja asked herself.

Chapter 24

Aaron watched Deja as she walked into the restaurant. Her hourglass figure looked perfect in the purple backless dress she wore. Her brown curls sat perfectly on her shoulders. She looked so elegant and beautiful. Aaron rose from his chair as she approached.

"You look gorgeous," Aaron said as he kissed Deja on the cheek.

"Thank you," she replied. He pulled out her chair for her and then tucked her in. Aaron sat down in his chair. For a moment, he just stared at Deja. She was so beautiful. He wondered what had taken him so long to make her his. "Aaron, stop staring." She giggled and tucked a lock of hair behind her ear.

"I can't help it," he admitted. Deja smiled shyly.

"Why is it so empty in here?"

"I asked them to close the restaurant down. I needed us to have privacy."

Deja raised her eyebrows. "Oh," She said. She looked so surprised.

"Did you like the flowers I sent you?" he asked. Deja burst out laughing.

"Yes, I did, thank you," she replied. "And now we're on our first date. You listened to me."

"I always listen to you."

Deja gasped. "No, you don't! You've cut me off on so many occasions," she said. Aaron grinned guiltily.

"From now on, I'll always listen to you," he said to her.

"You were so cold to me."

Aaron sighed. "It's not easy for me to just open up to people. I guess it comes off as being rude but it's not intended," he explained.

"I won't have to worry about you having an affair," Deja joked. Aaron smiled.

"Is that you agreeing to marry me?"

"No."

"I'll definitely convince you."

Deja raised an eyebrow. "How will you do that?" she asked.

"I have a few tricks up my sleeve." Aaron winked. Deja laughed and rolled her eyes. The waiters brought a selection of delicious foods. Aaron had picked the best restaurant in Al Nurat for their date. He wanted everything to go perfectly because he wanted to impress Deja. He wanted her to agree to marry him. She was beautiful, intelligent and amusing. She was the only woman that he had ever thought of marrying. And the thought of her being with another man didn't sit right with him.

After dinner, Aaron's driver took Deja and Aaron to the private airstrip. The car parked outside the jet. "What are we doing here?" Deja asked Aaron as they got out of the car.

"We're going to Bora Bora," Aaron said to her.

"What?" Deja spat out.

"Yeah." Aaron grinned.

"I haven't even packed anything." She looked so surprised.

"You won't need anything." Aaron whisked Deja into his arms. Deja let out a squeak and giggled. Aaron carried her to the jet.

***

It was a month later when Aaron and Deja returned to Al Nurat. It was the craziest thing that she had ever done; to just up and leave with a man. For one month, they had been traveling to different countries. During that time, they had done so many activities: swimming, fishing, hiking, horseback riding and so many other things.

Deja got to see a whole new side of Aaron. He had fully opened up to her. She learned about his childhood. He was raised to be a king. He was raised in a way that he wasn't meant to trust anyone. Upon learning this, Deja could understand why he wasn't as friendly. She was so happy that she had taken that vacation with him.

"Are you ready?" Aaron asked Deja as they walked into the palace.

"No, but we have to speak to your parents sooner or later," she replied. Aaron took her hand into his and kissed it. They headed to the king and queen's quarters. Deja knew that his parents were against them getting married. His mother had called him a couple of times and left messages. She wanted him to come home immediately.

Aaron's parents were sitting in their living room enjoying a hot cup of black tea when Deja and Aaron walked in.

"Oh my God," said the elegant older woman dressed in fine clothes and jewelry. She had a few grey hairs in her jet-black silky hair.

"You've decided to return," said the king. He wore a stern facial expression.

"And he brought *her* with him." The queen didn't look pleased to see Deja.

"Hello, your majesties." Deja bowed her head.

"Yes, I've brought her with me. I'd like to introduce her to you both as the woman I love," said Aaron. The king shook his head.

"Sit down," he said. "Both of you."

Aaron and Deja sat down at the sofas with Aaron's parents. Deja had never felt so nervous in her life before. She desperately wanted them to approve their marriage because she had never loved a man the way she loved Aaron. Her feelings for him had caught her off guard. When they first met, he was just a rude and cold man that she didn't understand. As they started to work together, she quickly developed respect and feelings for him.

"You say you love her?" the king asked Aaron.

"Yes, Father," Aaron replied.

"He's never loved anyone." The queen looked at her husband with concern.

"I've never loved anyone."

"Then how'd you know that you love her?" the king asked.

"I've never been interested in a woman for more than a week or two. No woman has ever challenged me as much as Deja has."

"And that's a good thing?"

Aaron nodded. "She makes me want to be the best man I can be. She inspires me, amuses me, annoys me and makes me happy. I can't imagine my life without her. The thought of her with another man makes my blood boil," he said. Both his mother and Deja gasped.

"That sounds twisted but I do believe that you love her," said the queen. The king whipped his head in her direction.

"Don't tell me you're going to let him marry her?" he said. The queen sighed.

"I'm just as unhappy about this as you are. However, Aaron has never been this interested in a woman. He even left the company for a month to go away with her. That's so unlike him," she said. The king grunted.

"Just what have you done to my son?" the king asked Deja.

"Your highness," Deja addressed the king. "I understand that I'm not Arabic nor am I the ideal woman for your son. However, I will strive to be. Please give us a chance to show you that we are meant for each other."

"Do you love my son?" the queen asked her.

"More than I've ever loved anything or anyone."

"The damage has already been done. He already told everyone that he is marrying Deja. There were cameras there." The queen shook her head. "We have no choice but to approve. We'd have to explain why he didn't marry her after announcing it."

Silence reigned in the room for a few minutes. "You have to learn Arabic and the culture," said the king.

"I am willing to learn," Deja replied.

"Fine." The king sounded so defeated. "I'll agree to this marriage on two conditions," he added.

"What are they?" Aaron and Deja asked at the same time.

"One; she will be vetted. I want to know everything about her from the moment she came out of her mother's womb. I don't want my daughter-in-law or her family to have a past that'll embarrass the royal family."

"I promise that you'll not find anything distasteful," said Deja.

"Two; I will give her two months to train. She must learn about our culture, language and history. And she must learn how to conduct herself as a queen," said the king. "If she fails one of these two conditions, then I'll not agree to this marriage."

Deja sighed with relief. "Thank you," she whispered as a tear rolled down her cheek. Aaron squeezed her hand and kissed it.

"Thank you," he said to his parents. "You won't regret this."

169

"We better not," said the king. The door swung open. Maria and Joseph walked into the room with smiles on their faces.

"Of course, the two of you were eavesdropping," said the queen.

"That was so intense," said Joseph.

"Welcome to the family," Maria said to Deja.

"Don't get too happy yet," the king said.

"She'll do great." Maria draped an arm over Deja and another over Aaron. "They make such a great couple. Thank you for approving the marriage. Two months to the wedding and eleven months to a grandchild!" added Maria.

"Hey, hold on! Grandchildren? We only just approved the marriage," said the queen. Everyone burst into laughter. Deja didn't mind that she had been given conditions. For Aaron, she'd do anything, even if his parents wanted her to wait two years. As long as his parents were agreeing to the marriage.

Deja looked at Aaron "I love you," she whispered.

"Ooooh, we all heard that! It wasn't quiet enough," said Maria with a wink. Everyone laughed at Deja.

"I love you too," Aaron declared loudly and kissed her.

What to read next?

If you liked this book, you will also like *In Love with a Haunted House*. Another interesting book is *The Oil Prince*.

In Love With a Haunted House

The last thing Mallory Clark wants to do is move back home. She has no choice, though, since the company she worked for in Chicago has just downsized her, and everybody else. To make matters worse her fiancé has broken their engagement, and her heart, leaving her hurting and scarred. When her mother tells her that the house she always coveted as a child, the once-famed Gray Oaks Manor, is not only on the market but selling for a song, it seems to Mallory that the best thing she could possibly do would be to put Chicago, and everything and everyone in it, behind her. Arriving back home she runs into gorgeous and mysterious Blake Hunter. Blake is new to town and like her he is interested in buying the crumbling old Victorian on the edge of the historic downtown center, although his reasons are his own. Blake is instantly intrigued by the flame-haired beauty with the fiery temper and the vulnerable expression in her eyes. He can feel the attraction between them and knows it is mutual, but he also knows that the last thing on earth he needs is to get involved with a woman determined to take away a house he has to have.

The Oil Prince

A car drives over a puddle and muddy water splashes Emily, who was just out for a walk, from head to toe. When she sees the car parked at a gas station moments later, she decides to confront the man leaning against it. The handsome man refuses to apologize, and after hearing what Emily thinks about him, watches her leave. The next day, fate plays a joke on Emily when she finds out that the man is her boss's brother and a prince of a Middle Eastern country. Prince Basil often appears in tabloids because of different scandals and in order to tame his temper, his father sends him to work on a project of drilling a methane well in Dallas. If Basil refuses or is unsuccessful, his financial accounts will be blocked and his title of prince will be revoked. Although their characters clash, Emily and Basil fall in love while working together and Basil's heart melts. When the project that can significantly improve his family business hits a major obstacle, Basil proves that love has tremendous power and shows a side of himself that nobody knew existed.

About Kate Goldman

In childhood I observed a huge love between my mother and father and promised myself that one day I would meet a man whom I would fall in love with head over heels. At the age of 16, I wrote my first romance story that was published in a student magazine and was read by my entire neighborhood. I enjoy writing romance stories that readers can turn into captivating imaginary movies where characters fall in love, overcome difficult obstacles, and participate in best adventures of their lives. Most of the time you can find me reading a great fiction book in a cozy armchair, writing a romance story in a hammock near the ocean, or traveling around the world with my beloved husband.

One Last Thing…

If you believe that *The Sheikh's Choice* is worth sharing, would you spend a minute to let your friends know about it?

If this book lets them have a great time, they will be enormously grateful to you – as will I.

Kate

www.KateGoldmanBooks.com